AF423560

Lovina's Amish Family Secrets

Tracy Boswell

Published by Trellis Publishing, 2021.

This is a work of fiction. Similarities to real people, places, or events are entirely coincidental.

LOVINA'S AMISH FAMILY SECRETS

First edition. July 13, 2021.

Copyright © 2021 Tracy Boswell.

ISBN: 979-8224710263

Written by Tracy Boswell.

LOVINA'S AMISH FAMILY SECRET

Tracy Boswell

Chapter One

"I didn't know you were back in town."

Lovina Miller turned to face the man who had spoken to her. He stopped a few feet away from her, amid the shelves of sundry items for sell at the Troyer & Hershberger Dry Goods Store.

The man stood a head taller than Lovina, and she guessed him to be about half a dozen years older than her own age of eighteen. He was dressed in a light blue button-front shirt, the sleeves rolled up to his elbows, and black trousers with suspenders. No hat covered his head, but a slight wave in his chestnut hair marked the place where one had sat earlier that day.

He looked familiar, and it only took her a moment to realize his identity. "Amos."

Although a dark beard obscured the lower half of Amos Troyer's face, it didn't hide the smile that curved up the corners of his mouth as his brown eyes lit with a warm expression. "Hello, Lovina. It's been a long while since I last saw you."

"Yes." It had been much too long since she'd left the small Amish community.

But it had not been by choice.

As a seven-year-old girl, Lovina hadn't been given a say in the matter. Her protests had made no difference.

She'd never understood why her mother had decided that they must move away and start a new life in Cincinnati after Lovina's father died. The older woman had grown up here on a farm a few miles outside of town, had never lived anywhere else prior to that. But any time Lovina tried to question her mother about it, she'd always changed the subject, refusing to discuss it.

Now that Lovina had return, she was hoping to find answers at last.

She had lived in Cincinnati almost twice as long as she'd lived here, so long that Amish words had completely disappeared from her speech—yet, this place still felt like home to her. And it always would. She knew that was partly due to the man standing in front of her.

Even as a boy, Amos had never been too busy to talk to her whenever they happened to meet. It hadn't mattered to him that she was five years younger than him. He'd always shown her kindness and often given her a bit of candy when she came into his family's dry goods store with her parents.

Thoughts of him had come to her at the most unexpected times while she struggled to adjust to life in the *Englisch* world. And it seemed that he had not forgotten her either, despite the years she'd been away.

The knowledge caused a curious sensation in her heart. "I'm surprised you recognized me. I'm sure I've changed a lot since then." Even though she was back in Amish clothes at last, she must look very different from the young girl he'd once known.

"I almost didn't recognize you," he admitted. His gaze swept across her face with an appreciative gleam. "You're grown up in the past eleven years."

Her cheeks heated in response to his words and the approving look in his eyes. "So have you."

She couldn't help noticing that he'd grown into a handsome young man.

Lines fanned out from the corners of Amos's eyes as his smile widened. "I'm glad you've finally come back for a visit. How long will you be in town?"

"Oh, I'm not just visiting. I'm living at the farmhouse now."

She didn't think it was her imagination that he appeared pleased by her pronouncement. And she hoped they would be seeing a lot more of each other in the days to come.

"Has your *maemm* returned here, as well?" Amos asked, breaking into her thoughts. "Or is she staying in Cincinnati?"

Lovina shook her head as sadness welled up inside her. "She passed away a few months ago."

There was nothing for Lovina in Cincinnati any longer, now that her mother was gone. The house they had lived in together had been rented, and she'd had no desire to renew the lease and continue living there alone.

She'd had no desire to remain in Cincinnati at all. The only thing that had kept her in the city after she'd turned eighteen was her mother's presence. But that was no longer a consideration.

Lovina had started making plans to return here shortly after the older woman had been laid to rest.

Compassion shone in Amos's eyes and he reached out to place a hand on her arm. "I'm sorry to hear of her passing."

Lovina took comfort from his consoling gesture, as she blinked back the tears that threatened to fall. "Thank you for your kind words, Amos. I wasn't certain whether you would still be working here at your father's store." Or if he might have moved away. "You appear to be doing well for yourself."

"*Yah*. I don't just work here, though. I own the dry goods store now. My *daed* passed away three years ago."

"I'm sorry to hear that," she repeated his words back to him.

Amos nodded in acknowledgement and his expression turned sad for a moment.

She knew well the pain caused by the loss of a parent. Even though Amos's loss was not as fresh as hers, the hurt still lingered.

She had hoped to speak to Amos's father, hoped that perhaps the older man could shed come light on the Christmas cards Lovina had found when she'd gone through her mother's things following her death.

Lovina had not realized that her mother had been in contact with anyone from the Amish community, but the bundle of Christmas cards proved otherwise. It was clear they had been written by a man who'd held a great deal of regard for the older woman. Lovina had been able to piece together the fact that the two had been involved in a romance before Lovina's mother had married her father.

The man had alluded to the reasons Ruth Miller moved to Cincinnati, but he'd never come right out and said why she'd insisted on leaving town.

The cards had only brought Lovina more questions than answers. Because none of them had been signed. The only clue she had to the sender's identity was the return address—Troyer & Hershberger's Dry Good Store.

Lovina wondered if the sender might be a clerk at the dry goods store. But he could just as easily be using the address to keep his true identity hidden. She wondered if Mr. Hershberger might be able to provide some information that would help her solve the mystery.

And then maybe Lovina would finally know why she'd been forced to leave the Amish way of life behind, forced to grow up in the *Englisch* world instead. A question that had haunted her for more than ten years.

"Is Mr. Hershberger still around?" she asked.

Amos shook his head. "Abram Hershberger passed away earlier this year."

"He's gone?" She was unable to keep the note of dismay from her voice as the words burst from her.

She hadn't known how much had changed in the years she'd been away. Perhaps it had been naïve of her to expect that everything here would have remained the same.

How would she ever get answers now? *Would* she ever get the answers now?

Amos seemed taken aback by her reaction to the news he'd imparted, his eyebrows knitting together in confusion. Which was not surprising since she hadn't been close to Mr. Hershberger.

She couldn't actually remember exchanging more than a handful of words with the older man. But then, why would he have any need to speak to a seven-year-old girl? Especially since he'd usually stayed on the farm where he lived with his wife and left the running of the dry goods store to Amos's father.

"I didn't realize you knew him that well," Amos said, his thoughts obviously traveling along the same lines as hers.

"I didn't, but..." She hesitated, wondering how much she should reveal to Amos.

She wanted to ask him a number of questions, but wasn't sure just how to go about it. Should she just blurt out everything? Or take a more circumspect approach?

"But what?" Amos prompted when the silence had stretched on between them for several seconds.

Lovina experienced a sudden moment of worry about what she might uncover if she continued down this path. There had to be a reason why her mother always refused to talk about it, after all. But Lovina would not let her doubts deter her from the search for answers. She wasn't willing to give up. Not until she learned the truth.

And that meant taking someone into her confidence. Who better than Amos, the boy who has shown her such kindness as a child?

She hadn't feel right contemplating giving him an evasive response anyway.

She explained about the Christmas cards her mother had received, and why she'd hoped to learn who had written the messages inside.

Amos listened without comment, and she couldn't tell from his expression what he was thinking.

"Do you know who might have sent the cards to my mother?" she questioned. "Are any of your male clerks the right age?"

* * *

Amos Troyer wished he could help Lovina Miller, but he was forced to shake his head in the negative to both her questions.

He had been only twelve when Lovina and her mother moved away from the Amish community. At that age, he hadn't paid much attention to the friendships and interactions between the adults living in the area. He'd never heard any talk of why Lovina and her *maemm* had left the Amish community. And he had no knowledge of anyone at the dry goods store sending cards over the past ten years.

Some days, it was hard to believe so much time had passed. Yet, other days it seemed like much longer than that.

Lovina was dressed in a plain navy blue dress and a white *kapp* covered her hair. The clothes were familiar, but not much else had stayed the same over the intervening years. Her hair had darkened from blond to light brown, and the freckles he remembered so well had faded from her skin. The one thing that remained unchanged was her bright green eyes.

After all this time, he hadn't truly expected to see her again. But he was glad she was back.

He had missed Lovina more than he had ever expected. Their age difference had seemed much more significant back then, and he wouldn't have called them friends. But he'd certainly noticed her absence when she was gone.

And he wanted to take away the look of dejection on her face now.

"Perhaps Mrs. Hershberger might be able to provide some answers," he suggested, mentioning Abram Hershberger's widow. "She still lives out on her family's farm several miles outside of town."

Lovina's mouth turned down at the corners. "It's a bit late in the day to walk that far. I had to walk into town since I don't have a horse, and the buggy in the barn at the farm is in need of repairs anyway."

"I could drive you out to the Hershberger farm," her offered.

"Don't you need to stay here and help customers?"

He waved away her concern. "I can take a break. Jacob's working today," he mentioned one of his clerks. "I'll just let him know that I'll be gone for a while."

Her frown disappeared to be replaced by a smile. "Thank you, Amos."

Lovina's bright smile brought a warm feeling to his heart. And he was looking forward to spending more time in her company.

Chapter Two

Lovina cleared her throat and shifted on the chair where she perched in Mrs. Hershberger's living room. Her discomfort was only partly due to the hard wooden chair, however. She didn't know whether she would have been able to find the courage to continue if Amos had not been by her side.

Talking to the stern-faced older woman was proving to be more difficult than she had anticipated, but she forced herself to forge ahead regardless.

In answer to Lovina's question, Mrs. Hershberger claimed to know nothing about the cards sent to Lovina's mother.

"Do you have any idea who might have written to her?" Lovina pressed.

The older woman's lips flattened into a thin line, and she shook her head sharply. "*Neh.* I'm wasn't close to Ruth Miller when she lived here. She certainly never shared any confidences with me. I'm ten years older than she was."

A sigh slipped from Lovina's lips. This was obviously a dead end.

"Perhaps it would be wise to stop poking into the past," Mrs. Hershberger advised. "No good can come of it, as my *daed* used to say."

"I don't think I can do that," Lovina replied. And what harm could it really do?

The older woman's face pinched up for a moment before she smoothed out her expression. "Well, you'll be returning to Cincinnati soon, and I'm sure that will put an end to it."

"I won't be returning to Cincinnati. I inherited the farm from my mother, and I'm living there now."

Mrs. Hershberger's eyes widened in surprise, but she didn't say anything more on the subject.

Once they left Mrs. Hershberger's farmhouse, Amos helped Lovina back into the buggy then climbed up on the seat beside her.

Taking up the reins, he set the horse in motion and they headed down the long dirt drive toward the highway. "I'll drop you off at your farm before I head back to the dry goods store."

She nodded in acknowledgement to his words, but didn't reply.

Amos shifted on the bench seat. "I'm sorry Mrs. Hershberger wasn't more helpful. But perhaps someone else in town can provide the answers you're searching for," he suggested in an encouraging tone.

"Perhaps." But she had to admit—if only to herself— that she was feeling rather defeated at the moment.

They were silent for several minutes until they reached the highway.

"What do you intend to do now that you've returned to the farm?" Amos asked over the sound of the horse's hooves clip-clopping on the pavement.

"The land has been leased to a neighbor for several years, but the farmhouse was neglected entirely since we left. It's going to need a good bit of repairs." She had spent several days cleaning, but there was still a daunting list of tasks left to be done.

"Have you hired someone to complete the work?"

"I can't afford to hire anyone since I only have the small income from renting out the farmland. I'll have to do everything myself."

Amos tugged on the brim of his hat to shade his eyes from the glare of the afternoon sun, then turned his gaze toward her. "I'd be glad to help you with that."

Her heart leaped at the thought of spending more time with Amos, but she didn't want to impose on him any more than she already had by allowing him to drive her out to the Hershberger farm. Which had turned out to be a completely pointless effort. It had brought her no closer to answering the question that had plagued her for so many years.

"Thank you for the generous offer, Amos, but I can't accept without giving something in return. Would you allow me help out at the dry goods store to repay you for your kindness? That is, if Mrs. Hershberger doesn't mind."

He cocked his head to the side, confusion plain in his dark gaze. "Why would she mind?"

Now Lovina was the one feeling confused. "Doesn't she own half the store since her husband passed away?"

"No, she didn't inherit it. I'm the sole owner now, though I decided to keep the Hershberger name on the sign."

"Oh, well then, will you let me help out at your store in exchange for lending a hand with the repairs to the farmhouse?"

"It's not necessary, but it sounds a fair trade." He squinted at the sun sinking toward the horizon. "I need to return to the store now. However, I could be at your farm early tomorrow morning."

She shook her head. "I'm still waiting on the lumber yard to delivery the wood I ordered to replace the rotted boards. It should arrive by the end of the week, though. Why don't I come by the dry goods store tomorrow and help you instead? And you can come by the farm in a few days."

He nodded in agreement. "I'll look forward to it."

A short time later, Amos pulled the buggy to a stop in front of Lovina's rundown farmhouse and came around to help her down. Once her feet touched the ground, he held on to her hand for a moment longer than was strictly necessary.

But she had no desire to pull away.

* * *

Amos forced himself to let go of Lovina's hand and turned to look at the farmhouse.

He'd driven past on the road at least a dozen times in the last year, but it was still a shock to see the deteriorated condition of the house close up. This would be more than just an afternoon of work—or even two or three days. Not that he had any intention of going back on his word. But there was no denying that it was a fair bit more than he had been expecting.

Of course, that meant he'd be spending much more time with Lovina than he had anticipated. A fact he was not at all unhappy about.

He shifted his gaze to Lovina and caught her grimace as she stared at the house.

Her teeth sank into her bottom lip, and her eyes met his. "I know it's in rough shape. If you want to withdraw your offer, I'll understand."

"*Neh*," he denied. He wasn't afraid of hard work. But he couldn't help asking, "Does the inside need as much work?"

"Not quite." Her expression seemed to belay her words, however. "Maybe you should come in and see what you're agreeing to before you make any promises."

"See what I'm getting myself into, you mean," he teased.

Her lips quirked slightly in response. "Something like that."

He followed her into the farmhouse and realized that she had not been overstating the amount of work that was required.

"Are you still willing to help me?" she asked when they were back outside once more.

"*Yah*." Nothing he had seen was enough to make him change his mind.

He doubted that *anything* would have been enough to make him turn down the opportunity to stay in Lovina's company. He felt an undeniable draw to her.

A smile lit her face. "Then, I'll see you tomorrow at the dry goods store."

Amos nodded in agreement, an answering smile on his face.

He could have happily remained with her for the rest of the day, but he had work waiting for him back at the store, so he forced himself to climb up into his buggy.

He touched the brim of his hat in parting. "Until tomorrow."

She waved to him as he turned the horse to start the return journey to town.

Chapter Three

As Lovina tried to fall asleep that night, thoughts of Amos filled her mind, keeping her awake. He was just as kind to her as he had been all those years ago. He'd grown into a good man, the type of man Lovina had always hoped to marry.

She drifted off to sleep dreaming of the loving family—a caring husband and several sweet children—that she prayed would live with her on the farm one day.

It seemed like only a few minutes later when she was jerked from a sound slumber by noises outside the farmhouse.

She lit the lantern on the nightstand and moved to the window to look outside. But she was unable to see anything in the darkness besides eerily shifting shadows.

The noises continued, sending a shiver down her spine.

She retuned to bed and wrapped the quilt tightly around her, trying not to think about how alone she was out here. She wasn't used to living in the country any longer, but that was no cause to let fear overwhelm her.

It's probably just the wind blowing a tree branch against the side of the house or an animal making those sounds, she reasoned.

Despite the perfectly logical explanation, she had a hard time falling back to sleep.

The sun had just risen when Lovina got out of bed the next morning and began to prepare for the day. After breakfast, she took a quick look around the outside of the farmhouse to see if she could spot the source of the noises that had kept her awake until shortly before dawn. Finding no signs of anything out of the ordinary, she again scolded herself for her unwarranted jumpiness.

She breathed in the fresh country air as she made the walk into town, marveling at how different it was from Cincinnati. She didn't miss the city at all.

It was good to be home, at last.

"Good morning, Amos," she said with a smile when she entered the dry goods store a short time later.

He returned her greeting, his brown eyes warming. "How are you this morning?"

"Fine," she replied, not making any mention of the noises that had frightened her the night before.

In the bright light of day, she felt more than a little silly for her overreaction.

Amos gave her a list of tasks, but remained nearby in case she ran into any difficulties. She enjoyed having him close—and it had nothing to do with worry that she might need to call on him for assistance with a customer.

Throughout the morning, a steady steam of people came into the store. Lovina renewed her acquaintance with friends and neighbors she had not seen in more than ten years. It seemed that everyone wanted to stop and chat with her, eager to hear all the details of her life in Cincinnati and what had brought her back to the Amish community.

She must have repeated the same handful of sentences at least a dozen times. As the hours passed, she worried that she was doing more talking than actual work. Thankfully, Amos didn't seem to mind.

She started asking questions while she was helping out at the dry goods store, hoping to discover the identity of the man who had sent her mother those Christmas cards. Though she was careful not to give any indication as to her true aim. She wasn't sure why she suddenly felt the need to hide certain facts. She didn't try to fight the inclination, however.

But no one she talked to seemed to know anything. Nor did they have any significant information to impart about Ruth Miller's reasons for leaving the community.

Or if they did, they weren't sharing it with Lovina. Maybe that was due to the fact she wasn't willing to ask direct questions that might give away more than she wanted to reveal. But she wasn't ready to give up yet.

As she continued to dig into the details of her mother's past, a few people suggested that the move to Cincinnati had been prompted by nothing more than the death of Lovina's father. But somehow, she couldn't quite believe that explanation.

So, what was the truth?

Would she ever find the answers she sought?

* * *

Amos enjoyed having Lovina helping out at the store. He liked having her near. He almost hoped the lumber shipment would be delayed, so that she would continue to come to his store and he would have an excuse to see her every day. And he wouldn't mind if the work at her farm took a good long time, too.

At the end of the week, Lovina approached Amos shortly after noon.

"I need to return to the farm. The lumberyard is going to deliver the wood I ordered this afternoon."

Although he was disappointed to see her go, he didn't try to convince her to stay. He nodded in acknowledgement to her words when he realized she was waiting for him to respond.

"Would you like me to drive you home?" He had made the offer every day this week, reminded of the long walk to reach her farm.

But just like every time before, she again refused now. "No. I'll be taking you away from the store enough while you're helping me work on the farmhouse. That is, if you're still willing."

"Of course I am. I'll come out to the farm tomorrow to start the repairs."

Warmth lit her eyes and a smile stretched across her lips. "If you come about eight o'clock, we can share breakfast before we get started."

Amos wasn't about to turn down that invitation. "I'll see you then."

As he watched her leave the store and walk down the street, he could hardly wait until the next time he would see her again.

The morning couldn't come soon enough for him.

Chapter Four

Lovina had a hard time sleeping that night, thinking about Amos's imminent arrival the next morning. She was eager for the sunrise, and eventually she fell asleep.

Pitch-blackness shrouded the bedroom when she was woken from a deep sleep by noises outside. It had been several nights since the last time, and she'd thought she had gotten over her irrational fear. But her suddenly clammy skin indicated otherwise.

You're being silly, she admonished herself. *There's nothing out there to be afraid of.*

She didn't bother to light the lantern and go to the window, since she wouldn't be able to see anything anyway. And no way was she going outside to investigate. Instead, she stayed tucked under the covers and tried to ignore the eerie sounds.

It was more than an hour later before she was able to get back to sleep.

After Amos arrived the following morning, they enjoyed breakfast together then headed out to the barn where the lumberyard had stacked the boards the previous day.

Expect there were no boards there when Lovina and Amos entered the dim interior.

Amos's brow wrinkled in confusion, but it was nothing to what Lovina was feeling.

"Did the lumberyard not make the deliver yesterday?" he questioned.

"No, I mean, yes, they did. I saw them unloading the wagon."

He turned in a circle, as though he expected the pile of wood to be hiding in a dark corner.

"Then where is it?" he asked when he faced her once more.

Bewilderment filled her. "I don't know." Suddenly, she remembered the noises that had awaken her the night before and a creeping suspicion entered her mind. "I think someone stole it."

He shook his head in disbelief. "Why would anyone in town do that? I can't imagine anybody I know stealing from a neighbor. Can you?"

"No, but..." Someone obviously had.

The wood was gone, and there was no explaining away that fact.

Amos glanced out the open barn doors toward the ramshackle farmhouse. "We won't be able to do the repairs until the lumberyard can send over another wagonload of boards."

A wave of turbulent emotion crashed over Lovina, but she tried to control it. "I'm sorry you came all this way for nothing."

"It wasn't for nothing," Amos replied. "I got to share breakfast with you, after all. That made the trip from town more than worth it."

She smiled in response, her cheeks heating at the soft look in his eyes. She suddenly felt a bit tongue-tied. Could he possibly feel the same affection for her that she felt toward him? She wasn't brave enough to ask him.

"This is only a minor setback," he assured her, unaware of the direction her thoughts had taken.

She was brought sharply back to the matter at hand.

She nodded in reply to his words, but she couldn't help wondering if it was much more than that, as her mood dimmed considerably at the reminder of the missing lumber.

Was it just a random occurrence? It seemed possible...except last night had not been the first time she'd heard noises in the darkness outside the farmhouse. What if the noises earlier that week hadn't been the wind or an animal as she'd worked so hard to convince herself?

Could both incidents be connected to the questions she'd been asking around town? She had tried to be subtle in her search for information. But when she first returned to the Amish community, she'd talked to Amos at the dry goods store where anyone could have overheard her. She hadn't held anything back, then. Unfortunately, she hadn't paid attention to who else might be around at the time.

Did someone not want her dredging up the past? Or did they not want her here at all? Was someone trying to chase her away?

Those thoughts were still circling in her mind a few days later when she returned to work at the dry goods store. But despite her worries, she couldn't stop her search for answers.

Lovina was in the middle of a conversation with a woman who has known her mother since she was a young girl. Lovina remembered the dark-haired woman visiting the farm often before they'd moved to Cincinnati.

The older woman opened her mouth to reply to a question when a stack of canned peaches suddenly toppled off the shelf behind Lovina and narrowly missed hitting her in the head. The metal cans made a loud racket as they landed on the hard wood floor.

Lovina's heart pounded in her chest at how close she had come to injury. Amos was there at once, asking her if she was all right. She nodded her head, but was unable to form any words.

Mrs. Hershberger suddenly appeared from the other side of the row of shelves. "Oh, dear, you'd best be careful or you'll be hurt."

Something about the older woman's concern seemed feigned, though Lovina couldn't be certain. Still, it raised a question in her mind.

Was the accident not an accident at all?

Chapter Five

The dark-haired woman excused herself, and Lovina and Amos bent to retrieve half a dozen dented cans that were scattered across the floor of the dry goods store.

All the while, Lovina considered the wisdom of continuing to search for answers someone clearly did not want her to find.

Amos picked up the last can and reached for Lovina's hand, helping her to straighten. "Are you certain you're all right?"

"Yes." She set an undamaged can back on the shelf. "I've decided to let the past rest."

She heard a noise behind her and turned to see that Mrs. Hershberger was still standing at the end of the aisle.

"Can I help you with something, Mrs. Hershberger," Amos asked.

"*Neh*. I have everything I need." She pivoted on her heels and exited the store.

Lovina couldn't help wondering if the older woman was responsible for all the misfortunes that had befallen her since she'd returned to town. But what possible motive could Mrs. Hershberger have to cause Lovina trouble? Yet, the suspicion remained.

Would the older woman stop now that she had heard Lovina say she was willing to leave well enough alone?

Even though the unanswered questions felt like a festering sore in her mind, she'd just have to resign herself to never knowing the truth.

Whether it had been Mrs. Hershberger to blame, or someone else, no further incidents occurred after that.

A new delivery arrived from the lumberyard a week later, and Amos returned to the farm to help Lovina with the repairs.

When she pulled away one of the rotted boards, she was surprised to find a diary hidden in the wall. As Amos continued to work, she opened the cover and realized the diary had belonged to her mother.

Lovina read an entry from the year before she was born and gasped in shock. "Did you know Mr. Hershberger and my mother...?" She couldn't find the words to finish the sentence. "Abram Hershberger was my father."

Amos narrowly avoided hitting his thumb with the hammer, but Lovina barely noticed. "My mother's family didn't approve of him. He didn't own the dry goods store then, and they thought he would never amount to anything. They arranged a match with a man they thought was more suitable." She flipped to a later entry in the diary. "Mr. Hershberger was the one who sent all those Christmas cards to my mother."

Astonishment suffused Amos's expression. "I didn't know. He never said a word about any of it to me."

She continued reading, then sighed as she closed the diary. "My mother decided to leave here to spare Mrs. Hershberger. Apparently she was worried that her husband would leave her to be with my mother after my father—I mean—" She cut herself off abruptly.

What was she supposed to call the man who had raised her, the man she'd always believed to be her father, now that she knew they were not truly related?

"I know who you mean," Amos said.

Lovina gave a jerky nod and continued. "After he died, my mother thought it would be better for everyone if she left."

She set the diary aside and walked outside, struggling to process everything she had just discovered.

How could her mother have kept the truth from her for all these years?

* * *

Amos followed Lovina outside a few minutes later and found her sitting on the front porch steps. "Do you mind if I join you?"

She shifted to make room for him and he sat down beside her. When she didn't say anything for several moments, he finally broke the silence.

"Are you all right?"

"Yes. I just...never expected to find out something like this. I thought—" she shook her head. "I don't know what I thought. I'm still having a hard time making sense of it all."

He wrapped an arm around her and she laid her head on his shoulder. They sat like that for a long while before Lovina straightened up and suggested they return to work.

Over the next few days, as they worked together to make the repairs to the farmhouse, Lovina talked openly to him about her feelings. She was slowly coming to accept things.

Amos was glad that she didn't have to go through this alone, that he was able to be here for her.

He wanted to be with her always. To build a life with her.

He found himself returning to a thought he'd had for the past several days, only this time he spoke it aloud. "Mr. Hershberger never had any other children. By rights you should own half of Troyer & Hershberger's Dry Goods Store, Lovina. I want you to be my partner."

Her eyebrows knit together above her green eyes. "Wouldn't that raise a lot of questions?"

"Not if you marry me."

She started to shake her head, but he stopped her before she could voice the refusal that he feared was on her lips.

"I don't just want you to be my wife because it's convenient, Lovina. I've fallen in love with you."

Sudden tears shimmered in her eyes, sparkling like dew on new spring leafs. "You love me?"

"*Jah.*"

Her eyes welled with more tears. "I love you, too."

He brushed away two teardrops as they rolled down her cheek. "Then can I assume these are happy tears?"

"Yes," she said with a laugh that rang with pure joy.

"And you'll marry me?"

"Yes, Amos. Nothing would make me happier."

A wide grin stretching across his mouth and he gathered her close for a kiss.

They would make the farmhouse a home. And one day they would pass the dry goods store to their children.

Until then, Amos was looking forward to sharing many wonderful years with Lovina. Working side by side together.

* * * * *

The End

AN AMISH GIRL IN NEW YORK

It had taken months of begging and pleading to Mama and Papa, but they finally gave in. Ever since she was a little girl, Abby had an obsession with New York City. There was something about its bustling streets, towering buildings, and even its grit and grime that was so opposite to her small Amish community out in the countryside that unrelentingly called out to her. Each time her family passed through neighboring towns on their way to some market or trade show, she'd soak up every billboard and image depicting the towering skyline of the city that never sleeps.

Abby's parents always thought of her fascination with the city as a passing phase, something all young girls go through in some form or another, but once she turned sixteen she began talking more seriously about leaving home. Mama and Papa went away on rumspringa themselves when they were around her age, but they were still nervous thinking about their only daughter running off to the big city. At first, they insisted she pick a smaller, less intimidating city to visit, like Philadelphia or even Chicago where they had family that could keep on eye on her, but Abby was relentless. They tried to convince her to wait until her younger cousin was old enough to go with her to no avail. Abby had been waiting to go to New York City for as long as she could remember and once she turned eighteen she decided she couldn't wait a single second longer.

That morning, bags packed and dressed for travel, Abby sat down at the breakfast table and told her parents that she was leaving that day, with or without their permission. Not wanting to harbor any ill feelings toward their daughter or to explain to their neighbors that she ran off against their wishes, Mama and Papa gave in with a collective defeated sigh. Abby jumped up like a shot and hugged both her parents at once, almost knocking them to the floor.

"Thank you, thank you, thank you! I promise I'll be okay. Sarah's cousin has an apartment in Manhattan and she said I could stay with her for as long as I want and you don't even have to worry about money because Sarah says everyone in New York serving food at restaurants and it would be super easy for me to get a job, even without any experience or anything. I'll write to you every day, or every other day, or when I have time. It's New York, after all. I'm going to have so much to do! It's all so exciting!"

Abby flashed her parents a bright, enthusiastic smile that they tried to replicate, but their nerves stood in the way. Sarah was Abby's best friend from school. Her parents never let her go on rumspringa because of her cousin, Grace. Grace left home to visit the city when she was eighteen and never came back. Sarah's family was devastated, but Sarah kept in touch with Grace and was assured that she was happy and had made the right choice. Sarah's parents didn't want to take the risk that she might do the same.

"Just...be careful. Remember what you have waiting for you back at home."

"Listen to your Mama. This will always be your home. God has a path set for you here."

Abby brushed off her parents' words of caution with a closed-lipped smile and a small shrug. She understood their concern, but a week, or month, or year in New York wouldn't change her fundamental beliefs, and if it did would that automatically be a bad thing? Grace has lived in New York and away from the church for five years now and she was still a good person. Why did being Amish mean she had to hide herself away from the rest of the world her whole life? If she didn't go see the city she's dreamed of her entire life now then she never would. Besides, she was pretty sure she'd come back home. Her parents shouldn't worry so much.

Mama and Papa insisted she stay for one last meal before she caught the bus one town over that said "New York City" on the front. Abby could barely sit still long enough to bring bites of food to her mouth without shaking them off her fork. She'd seen that bus come and go hundreds of times, but that was the day she'd be going with it. Her mother tried to keep up a normal conversation, but Abby could only respond with "yes" or "no." Her mind was officially elsewhere. Eventually her father excused her from the table and she almost ran right out the door, but a small pang in her stomach stopped her at the threshold. Abby was unquestionably excited to start her journey, but she realized that she would miss her parents along the way. She slowed down for a moment to hug them both goodbye.

"Mama, Papa, I love you both very much. I'll see you when I get back."

She added that last part mostly to reassure her parents, but also a little bit for herself. She'd always imagines what might happen if she decided to stay in New York. She'd work hard to become an actress on Broadway, and one night a handsome fan would come to her dressing room after a particularly stirring performance and confess his love for her. It would turn out that he came from a rich family, of course, and even though she could absolutely support herself being a successful actress and all, she'd be in love and carefree for the rest of her life in a Manhattan penthouse. That was all a harmless fantasy, but the walk to the bus stop was absolutely real. An ounce of nervousness mixed with the excitement swirling around in her head.

She made it just on time, walked on to the half-filled bus, handed her ticket to a stone-faced bus driver and found a seat by the window. She wanted to see every inch of the city as they drove into it. An older woman with a lap full of knitting sat next to her and smiled. The familiarity calmed her a bit. Her mother spent the weekends knitting one and purling two after the morning's chores were finished. It would be a few hours before the skyline even came into view and the slow rocking of the bus soon lulled Abby to sleep.

Two or three hours later, she wasn't sure exactly, a particularly large bump in the road jostled Abby awake. The woman next to her was still knitting what now looked like a child-sized sweater. A quick look out the window revealed the view she'd been dreaming of for eighteen years. Abby clutched the small backpack she brought packed full of all her possessions to her chest and gasped. It was exactly like the pictures, but it also wasn't. Nothing could have prepared her for the jagged line of towering buildings that rose up out of the ground in front of her. The old woman chuckled.

"First time in New York City, dear?"

"Is it that obvious? I've always wanted to visit, but this is the first time my parents actually let me on a bus."

"Well, I prefer the quiet of the country now, but I spent a fair amount of my younger years wandering through the city streets. My daughter lives in Manhattan, so when I visit I get live vicariously through her. I can never stay for too long, though. These old bones can't withstand the hustle and bustle like they used to. Stay out all night for me at least once, will you? There's nothing like Times Square once all the tourists have gone back to their hotels."

Abby tried to assure her that she was going to do everything in New York, especially Times Square, but the woman seemed to lose herself in the memory, smiling down at the knitting in her lap. Abby didn't mind the sudden end to their conversation, it only assured her that sometimes just thinking about being in New York City was better than whatever you were actually doing. Her nails dug into the sides of her backpack as she tried to contain her excitement.

Sarah had given Grace all of Abby's bus information: bus number, time of departure and arrival, where it was going to drop her off. She promised to meet her there and help her figure out the subway.

"I can probably do it on my own. She don't have to go out of her way," Abby had said to Sarah, but Sarah said Grace had laughed kindly and told her there was no way she was going to let an Amish teenage girl get lost in New York on her very first day.

"She might end up wandering around Coney Island and I won't have that."

The streets started to narrow as the bus made it's way deeper into the city and closer to their destination. They passed small corner stores with yellow banners marked "Deli Grocery," and pop-up street vendors selling flowers or fruit or both. Abby tried to remember the face of every new person she saw. Everyone was so different here than in her homogeneous Amish community back home and she loved it. Each unique face had a different story behind it. What did the woman without shoes dressed all in tie-dye do all day? What about the old man in a crisp, tailored suit who read a book while he walked? She loved this city and she hadn't even stepped off the bus yet.

At the bus stop, she recognized Grace right away. Not only could she have been Sarah's somehow older twin, but she was also holding a big poster board sign that said, "Welcome to the Big Apple, Little Amish Girl!" Grace must have recognized her, too, because the moment Abby stepped off the bus she sprinted over and wrapped her in a huge hug, dropping the poster into the street.

"You're finally here! Welcome, welcome, welcome! I'm so excited to have someone from back home come visit me. I love it here, but there's something comfortable about that little town, huh? You excited? You ready for your stay at Casa de Grace?"

Abby knew Grace was kind and outgoing from Sarah's descriptions of her, but she had no idea how energetic she was. Going from the quiet, slow-talking lifestyle back home to Grace's immediate exuberance matched only by the city's chatter behind her was a little overwhelming for her. She could only manage an enthusiastic smile and nod while stumbling over the words, "Yes, okay, I'm ready!" Grace released her from the hug, picked up her sign with one hand, and locked hands with Abby with the other. Abby watched Grace's free-flowing curly hair bounce along behind her as she chatted about everything she wanted to do together while Abby was here. She had dyed it red and let it loose after moving to the city, and Abby admired it. Her dusty blonde locks were almost always pinned tightly to the back of her head and hidden under a bonnet. She left the bonnet at home this time, but the pins remained. She wondered if Grace would help her dye her own hair, maybe black, or blue even. Her parents would love that.

Grace excitedly rattled on about Strawberry Fields in Central Park, and eventually making it to the Statue of Liberty because she hasn't been there in ages, and of course they had to see a Broadway show, there were supposed to be a couple good ones premiering soon, never letting go of Abby's hand. A couple of blocks later, they descended into a subway station and stopped at an automated kiosk to purchase a MetroCard. Abby had never interacted with a machine this complex before and almost froze, not quite knowing what to do with the ball of crumpled bills in her hand. Luckily, Grace was quick to remember what life back home was like and thoughtfully helped her through the process. Holding the bright yellow and blue card in her hand made her feel very grown up and independent. She even made it through the turnstile on the first try.

"You're a natural, Abby! You were made for New York," exclaimed Abby.

Maybe I am, Abby thought.

Mama and Papa may have had more to worry about than a daughter with blue hair.

Grace took a break from listing every attraction in New York City to look down at her cell phone as they took their seats. Abby wrapped her arms tightly around the backpack on her lap and looked around the half-filled car. The subway was a completely new experience for her. She had never been on a bus before, either, but she had seen buses and the types of people on them. *This is like, an underground bus,* she told herself, not completely comfortable with being so far beneath the earth. She focused on the other people sharing the car. Just like the people on the street, no two of them were exactly the same. A tattooed mother sat quietly bouncing a child in her lap, while a teen a few seats down mirrored that image with a boom box blaring hip-hop.

Abby jumped as the train began to move. Grace chuckled and put a hand on her arm.

"I did the same thing on my first subway ride. Turned out I was on the right train but headed the wrong way so I had bigger fish to fry than dealing with being on a train for the first time," she threw back her head and laughed at the memory. "Once I realized I was no where near where I wanted to be I got off the train and started asking people which train would take me where I needed to be and they just kept telling me the one I was on. I didn't realize that the train going in the right direction was just on the other side of the platform. Man, did I feel dumb, but you won't have to worry about that, you have me!"

The two girls chatted for a little while as the train made it's way to their stop. Once they emerged back onto the city streets Abby began to get a feel for the constant flow of people. She quickened her pace to match Grace's and only bumped shoulders with a handful of people as she weaved through the crowd. Eventually, they walked into a tall building where a man sat at a desk by the door.

"Morning, Fred! This is my, well, she's basically my cousin. Abby's gonna be staying with me for a while so don't surprised if she comes flying through here at all hours of the day, okay?"

"Not a problem, Gracie! A friend of yours is a friend of mine. Nice to meet you, Abby!"

Abby smiled and waved at him as they walked to the elevator. She was surprised at how friendly everyone seemed to be. On the odd occasion that she did get her parents to talk with her about New York all they had to say about it was how unwholesome and rude the people were. She'd have to tell them how wrong they were when she got back. *If* she went back.

"That's my doorman, Fred. He's awesome. Always happy to see you even in the middle of the night. If you get yourself locked out or something and I'm not around Fred will help you out."

"That's good to know, thanks. Is everyone in New York this friendly?"

Grace laughed again.

"Not at all. Don't get me wrong, you'll find friendly people if you look for them but a lot of people would run you over with their cars and never look back. They're not bad people, they just have things to do and places to be and no time to stop and check if you're alive or not. That's your problem."

Grace saw a look of dismay cross over Abby's face.

"Don't worry, though. I'll make sure to introduce you to all the best people in New York. You just make sure not to get hit by any cars."

The elevator dinged as they made it to the fourteenth floor. Grace's apartment was at the end of the hall. It had two bedrooms, both with views overlooking the busy streets below, a small kitchen, a bathroom to share, and a living room filled with paintings and posters and a million other colorful decorations. Abby noticed a picture of Grace and Sarah from years ago sitting on a table by the couch. Before she could walk over to get a better look, Grace waved her into one of the two bedrooms. The room had a few pieces of art on the walls, but wasn't near as covered as the living room. A small bed was pushed up against the wall and dresser sat across from it with a TV placed on top.

"This is your room! I moved a bunch of stuff out of it and into the living room so you wouldn't be overwhelmed. I've only been here for a couple of years but I've managed to collect so much junk. I guess that's what happens when you go from a simple Amish life on the family farm to the big city. I can show you how to use the TV, too. I wouldn't blame you if you spent your first couple of days here just sitting in front of it watching cartoons. I know I did."

It was tempting, but Abby had been waiting to be a part of this city for so long she almost felt cooped up just being in the room to drop her things off.

"I'll definitely watch some TV later, but right now all I want is to explore or maybe find I job. I promised my parents I wouldn't ask them for money."

"Oh! I forgot to tell you. I know the manager of the diner down the street. He said he was looking for waitresses so I told him about you. He wants you to come down tomorrow morning so he can make sure you're not a total klutz or anything but you've basically got the job! How do you feel about pancakes?"

"I love pancakes! Thank you so much, Grace. You've done too much already."

"Don't even worry about it. I know what it's like being cooped up on a farm with no electricity or entertainment or fun. I want to make sure you're trip is the complete opposite of that! All fun, all the time. So, what do you want to do first?"

They spent the rest of the day just walking around Manhattan. They stopped for coffee at a sidewalk café, bought a few outfits fit for work at a department store, watched the dogs run around at the dog park. It was a fairly average day in New York but to Abby it was the best day of her life. Grace was a wealth of information, only stopping the flow to take sips of her latte. She knew the best place to get a burger, the best place for live music, the best cup of coffee – this wasn't it, but it would do.

"It's almost dinner time so why don't we start with the best Chinese takeout and spend the evening just hanging out at my place. How does that sound? You must be exhausted!"

She was exhausted, but she'd never admit it. She could only agree that Chinese food did sound good, even though she'd never had it before, and she wouldn't mind a night in. They stopped at a hole-in-the-wall restaurant only distinguishable by its vaguely oriental décor. Grace never once looked at the menu as she rattled off a list of food: crab rangoons, fried rice, sweet and sour chicken, lo mien, and don't forget the fortune cookies! When they got back to the apartment, Grace spread the feast out on her coffee table, handed Abby a pair of chopsticks, and said "Dig in!" After some fumbling with the sticks, she was able to shovel mountains of delicious and greasy food into your mouth.

While they watched the movie "Mean Girls," one of Grace's favorites, Abby broke open a fortune cookie. One side listed a handful of lucky numbers and the other said, "A big surprise is coming your way." She had spent so much time planning for this trip, accounting for every little detail, she wondered what surprises the city could possibly have in store for her. She could hardly sleep that night thinking about it. Maybe she wouldn't get the job. Maybe New York wouldn't live up to her expectations, but that couldn't be it because they already had. Maybe it would be something else, something so surprising that she couldn't even imagine it yet. She hoped that was it.

***

In the morning, Grace woke Abby up with a gentle shake and a steaming cup of coffee.

"Morning sunshine! It's your first day of work and I don't want you to be late. Here, I made you some coffee and I picked out an outfit for you last night, but you don't have to wear it. Sorry I'm acting like such a mom after you came all this way to get away from your parents. Yikes!"

Abby laughed, "I wasn't running *away* from my parents, I was running *to* New York! Thank you for the pleasant wakeup call."

"Well, I was definitely running from my parents. Living in that house was stifling; all those rules, no fun, and for what? God's plan? Sorry, I just get a little frustrated sometimes thinking about all the things my parents kept from me back home. I still feel religious from time to time, but the rigid rules of Amish life just aren't for me."

"Yeah, I know what you mean. I feel like there's so much I want to do that I just can't there. That's why I wanted to come here. I want to get it all out of my system so that I can go back to living simply. Once I've done everything I'll probably be so exhausted that I'll want to go back anyways!"

Grace smiled at her kindly, but bit her tongue. She knew better than most that it didn't always work that way. She didn't want to influence Abby's choice either way, but life as she saw it couldn't just be flushed out of someone's system. A person either craves an Amish life, or an English one. Abby just had to decide which it was she wanted most.

"We can talk about the serious stuff later. Why don't you jump in the shower and get ready for work while I cook breakfast. Go ahead and use whatever you find in there. Mi shampoo es tu shampoo!"

Abby washed herself, changed into the clothes Grace picked out for her, and played around with her makeup. Back home she didn't have any of this stuff. You didn't need makeup to go to church. Plus, every boy she knew had known her since they were children. They'd just be confused if she showed up to the Sunday sing one day covered in powders and creams, but here, no one knew her. She could wear as much or as little makeup as she wanted and no one would question it. Abby decided to start small, only applying a small amount of blush and a couple coats of mascara. The thick frame of lashes made her eyes look huge and the soft pink on her cheeks gave her the appearance of being a little bit warm. Even this small amount of makeup looked jarring in the mirror, but she also kind of liked it.

When she finally emerged from the bathroom Grace was dancing around her kitchen using a spatula as a microphone. At the end of an exaggerated spin she saw Abby standing in the hall giggling.

"Hey! You look awesome! You even threw on some makeup? That's advance level stuff. Now you just need to learn to flirt a little bit and you'll be swimming in tips."

"I know how to flirt!" Abby said defensively.

"Ha! Staring at a boy across the room during prayer is not flirting. New York's a completely different world."

"Oh yeah? How different can city boys be?"

"You know what? You might be right. All you have to do is blink those big doe eyes at one of these too-cool-for-school guys and they'll be smitten. You'll do fine."

"I don't even know if I want to date anyways."

"Oh, you'll change your mind the first time a cute boy tells you he likes your smile. Trust me. It happens to the best of us."

They talked a little bit about boys and back home over breakfast before it was time for Abby to head to the diner. It was so close to Grace's apartment building that she brought Abby down to the lobby, pointed to the place on the corner, sent her on her way and told her to ask for a man named Greg. She was a little nervous to go on her own, but this was exactly the experience that she was hoping to have in New York. Abby craved a taste of independence and she was finally getting it.

The diner was called "Rizzo's Place" and it looked exactly how she'd pictured a classic New York diner. The tables and chairs were all covered in turquoise vinyl complete with little flecks of glitter and the wait staff were all wearing crisp white aprons and matching paper hats. The aprons reminded her of her mother's back home, but that was the only ounce of familiarity she felt. The restaurant was fairly busy. Early morning was their rush hour, but that had passed so only a handful of stragglers and early lunch-eaters remained. She was standing by the doorway when a man only a little older than her wandered over to see if she wanted a table.

"Hey there! Can I help you?"

"I'm looking for Greg. I'm supposed to start working today."

The man's face broke out into a huge smile and he leaned in for a hug.

"You must be Abby! Grace told me all about you and how hardworking and great you are. Grace and I are like this," he crossed his fingers to show that they were close, "so I'd do anything for that girl. Oh! I'm Greg by the way."

Abby gathered from his tone that he might be gay. She had met one gay boy before back in her town, but he hadn't told anyone aside from her and a few friends about his sexuality. It wasn't something that bothered her, but seeing a man so openly flamboyant surprised and encouraged her. She had always thought of New York as a place where everyone could be exactly who they wanted to be, and seeing this man live up to that ideal was exciting. Abby smiled back and nodded.

"That's me! Thank you so much for giving me this job."

"You're so cute! Abby, you're going to fit in just fine here. I almost don't even think I have to train you. Want to just throw on an apron and dive right in?"

When a nervous look crossed over Abby's face he added, "All you have to do first is introduce yourself and ask if they'd like anything to drink. They usually just want coffee or water. If they want coffee make sure to ask about cream and sugar. I'll only give you one table for now so don't worry! If you flop, I'll be here to help you out but you seem like a natural!"

Greg scoped the restaurant to see which table he wanted to throw at her.

"Okay, there's one guy sitting in the corner. He's a regular. He usually just comes in for a coffee, sometimes scrambled eggs with a side of bacon, but nothing too complicated. Nice guy. Are you ready?"

Abby nodded. Greg smiled and gently pushed her forward. She didn't realize how quickly she'd be thrown into the actual serving part of the job, but she wasn't about to embarrass herself so she threw back her shoulders and approached the table as confidently as she could.

"Hey there! I'm Abby. Can I get you a coffee to drink? I mean, can I get you anything?"

From far away she couldn't tell how subtly attractive the man in the booth was. He was partially hidden by a beanie hat and an oversize sweatshirt, but when she got closer Abby could see a sharp jaw line and kind eyes beneath the baggy outerwear. She was thrown off by her attraction for a moment, but her desire to impress her new boss prevailed. She flashed him a professional smile as she bit her tongue.

"Yeah, sure, a black coffee would be great."

"Can I get you anything else?"

"Not right now, thanks."

She turned on her heal and walked back to Greg, not sure where she was supposed to take the order. Luckily, he was watching enthusiastically from the sidelines cheering her on silently.

"How'd it go? Was he nice? What am I saying, he's always nice! What did he order?'"

"Just a black coffee."

"Yep, that sounds like him. Let me show you where the coffee station is."

Greg helped her find the station and pour a cup. He showed her where the cream and sugar was, just in case her next customer needed it. He then showed her how to use the computer system in order to keep track of what each customer ordered. This was all very simple, however, and it wasn't long until she was right back at her only customer's table with the cup of coffee.

"Here you are, sir. One cup of black coffee."

"Thanks, but why are you talking like that. It sounds like you're a robot who was programmed to work in a diner."

Abby blushed.

"Oh, well it's my first day. Sorry. I'm still trying to get the hang of things."

The customer looked a little embarrassed as well. He didn't mean to call her out.

"No, I mean, I'm sorry. I didn't mean to embarrass you. Thanks for the coffee. It's great, as always."

Abby gave him a polite, but uncomfortable, half smile and turned to walk away but he stopped her.

"Wait, what's your name?"

"Abby."

"Abby, like Abigail?"

"No. Just Abby, actually. My mom just liked Abby."

"That's a nice name. Mine's Mac, like Mackenzie. My mom wanted a girl, but got me instead, so she picked a gender-neutral name. I don't mind it, though."

"I like Mac. There aren't a lot of guys where I'm from with names like that."

"Oh yeah? Where is it that you're from?"

"It's a little Amish town just outside of here, actually. I just got into the city yesterday."

"Yesterday? You need someone to show you around then."

Abby blushed again. She thought about what Grace said about flirting for tips, but this felt more genuine than that. This guy, Mac, didn't seem to care about tips.

"I'd like that."

"Great! Give me your phone number and I'll call you up sometime."

"Oh, I don't have a phone number. I don't have a phone."

"That's right. The whole 'Amish' thing. Well, when do you get off here?"

Greg had been listening in the whole time and jumped into the conversation.

"Right now! She's done for the day, wasn't she amazing? I just have to teach her how to clock out and she'll be on her way!"

Greg pulled Abby to the side to chat, but Abby was confused.

"Did I do something wrong? Do you not want me to work here?"

"No! No, of course not. I've just seen this guy come in day in, day out and, don't get me wrong he's one of the nicest customers we have which is why I'm doing this, but he's never once brought in a date or left with one. It's just so cute seeing you two together I can't resist! Go! Have a good time and come back tomorrow and we'll give you some real training. It was my mistake for giving you the cute, single guy as your first table."

Abby almost didn't know what to do. She expected to start her first job, but instead she was going on her first date. She walked back over to Mac's table, Greg casually waving his hands to encourage her.

"Sorry about that. It looks like I'm free now."

"Great! I can take you to work with me then."

Abby had no idea what this entailed but Greg gave her a thumbs up and she followed Mac out of the diner. They walked for a few blocks, casually chatting about their lives. Mac was very interested in Abby's Amish community and Abby was very interested in where Mac was taking her. If it hadn't been for Greg's insistence, she probably wouldn't have felt comfortable following a man she just met through New York City, but she couldn't resist. Eventually, he led them into a building and up a few flights of stairs. Greg pulled back a sliding iron door to reveal a colorful studio filled with paintings and sculptures.

"This is where I work, and live, I guess."

"You're an artist!" Abby exclaimed.

"I'd like to think so, but I've been in a rut lately. I haven't been able to create anything new. I don't want to sound cliché, but would you mind if I tried painting you? You haven't even taken off your work apron yet and your eyes are just so beautiful."

He didn't comment on her smile, but Grace's words still ran through her mind as this boy asked if she'd model for him. On one hand, she was weary, but on the other his sincerity penetrated through most else. She didn't feel as though he wanted anything from her except for her image so she agreed. Mac and Abby sat mostly still for the next couple of hours as Mac swept acrylics across a large canvas, capturing Abby in that moment. When the painting was finally done he turned it around and approached her.

"Alright, here it is. How do you like it?"

Abby looked at herself, carefully depicted in paint. Mac had noticed her mascara covered eyes, but hadn't painted them in a cartoonish way. He'd only enhanced the features on her face that had already been beautiful.

"It's...gorgeous! Is that conceded to say?"

"No, not when you look like you do."

Mac leaned towards Abby to kiss her. She almost turned away, but her instincts took over. With his mouth on hers she finally felt free of her parents grasp and also just free in general. He pulled away before she was finished enjoying the moment.

"I don't want to overstep my boundaries here. I like you a lot, but where from two different worlds."

Abby smiled confidently for the first time and touched his face.

"This is exactly what I want," she said before leaning back in to finish the kiss.

***

The two teens dated for a few weeks after that first studio session. Abby posed for multiple paintings, some more revealing than others, but always with her expressed consent. She loved having her freedom. She loved being able to come and go from Grace's apartment as she wished, but eventually she got bored. One night, as Mac painted Abby holding a bouquet of roses while sitting on a couch, she finally hit her breaking point. She threw the roses up into the air and started to shout.

"Mac! I can't do this anymore. What's the point of me coming here, day after day, just to be your model?"

"You're gorgeous, Abby. You're my muse!"

"But what am I getting out of this? Where does this take me?"

Mac couldn't answer that and Abby got up to leave.

"This has been fun, Mac, but I don't have a purpose here. I think I need to go home."

Mac tried to convince her to stay. He tried to convince her that her portraits meant more to him than just simple trinkets, but she wasn't swayed. As fun as the city was, as much freedom as she had, home would always be back in her little farm town. God had always had a path laid out for her, and this turned out to be only a detour.

MY AMISH VISIT

SHELLY MARTIN

I drove by an old torn up sign that read "Sugar Grove, Pennsylvania: Population 566." I turned down two side streets and made a left on Trout Avenue before I found a beautiful yellow cottage that sat on Danbury Lane.

There were vines growing up the cottage and there was a small swing that sat by an old oak tree. I looked over at the neighboring farms and saw cows grazing in the fields nearby.

I didn't come to this small town to find a cowboy, I came here because I wanted to feel...something.

Something for my birth mother.

I slaved many late night hours working as a waitress at a small diner making trash for tips. I went to college then got a job at a newspaper.

All I did was study and work. I don't have a boyfriend.

I am different from most women my age. I don't party, don't curse and don't sleep around. Something always off and when I learned about the background of my birth mother things started to make sense.

I do believe that there are things we inherit from our parents other than physical characteristics. I believe we got some kind of a spiritual DNA.

I found out that my birth mother came from a community that doesn't use technology but remain tight-knit and look out for another with old-fashioned values.

Which brings me back to my siutation.

I had been feeling lonely. Most of my friends have gotten married and have children. I was a lost cause, I guess. I chose the single life over changing diapers. I gained some weight and some may say I did this to keep men away. Maybe that's true.

I like men and want to be married like my friends. But somewhere along in my journey I shut off my feelings.

My boss picked up on it. He told me that I was like an onion and not in a good way. My layers are thick and under ripe.

He told me to take a vacation. Find true emotion. If I did that, my writing would improve.

So now, I am here in the Amish community of Sugar Grove.

I walked through the door of the cottage expecting pictures of Jesus wall to wall. Instead, everything was painted a sky blue and trimmed in white. The pictures on the wall were of sunflowers and honeybees.

I expected to see a television but didn't. A small dining room table separated the two rooms. At the back of the cottage was a large bedroom. The room held a king size feather bed with all white linen, a large chest of drawers holding a large mirror. In front of the mirror were empty storage containers that were to be filled with my belongings.

In the kitchen, I noticed a note hung on the fridge. The owners said that my office called and arranged for the refrigerator to be stocked with foodstuff. I called my boss and thanked him for the kind gesture.

I milled around the cottage the rest of the evening and shot off a few e-mails before I went to sleep.

The next day I headed into town to stake out the local bakery. The front of the building had a sign that read, "Amish Bakery founded in 1848 by Tobias Hochstetler."

The structure was crafted out of natural wood and the window panes had flower boxes carved into them. The word "Bakery" was crafted out of white wooden blocks and plastered on the side of the building.

I smelled treats baking indoors and that was where I wanted to be. Bread? Cakes? What was that smell?

Another whiff told me that stew was simmering in pots on the stove in the back. I found a small table the rear of the bakery. I looked around for a plug but remembered that the Amish had no power.

I took my tablet and went on battery power, writing down my observations.

I took notice that people were walking through the doors and taking seats at various tables. The female patrons were dressed in calf length dresses that were of a solid color. They wore blue, purple and green dresses. Black bonnets over a white prayer cap. The men wore white shirts and dark pants with suspenders. When they entered they removed their hats and placed them on a rack in front of the bakery entrance.

It was only a matter of time before the place was almost full. I couldn't figure it out but there was something strange. Then it hit me.

The quietness of it all.

Everyone appeared to be either being working as a team or speaking in hushed tones. The employee's smiles appeared genuine as they greeted each table. I was amazed at how different service was compared to back in the city where people were shouting and their children were climbing over the tables.

The waiter came up to my table and greeted me as he did the others. I couldn't help but notice his sea green eyes and nice smile. His hair was cut into a shaggy style and his front tooth was slightly out of line. His skin held a golden hue from signaled he must always work long hours in the sun.

"Hello, my name is Abraham," he said, clearing his throat. "I'll be taking your order this morning, are you ready to order?"

"I'll take the breakfast puff," I said, stumbling through my words. "A banana. A cup of coffee. And a sugar cookie. And an oatmeal cookie. And the brown sugar cookie."

I didn't realize what I pig I must have sounded like but he just nodded his head as he took my menu and stepped away.

I groaned in embarrassment as I began writing on the tablet again.

"Oink, oink," I wrote. "Oink, oink.Way to impress a cute Amish boy."

Losing focus, I watched as the other patrons spoke so quietly that I had to strain my ears to hear what they were saying. When their food came, they said a word of prayer and ate in total silence.

Abraham brought my order and asked, "Is there anything else I can do for you?"

"No, thank you."

I glanced back and watched him walk away. I found that the service staff never left the front of the business. They stood at a podium and waited for tables that needed to be serviced. If a patron looked up the waiter was immediately there. No food was sent back and as the patrons left they all thanked the chef in German. I learned "denki" meant thank you and was pronounced "den-gee." Every single table wished to speak with the baker. At first, it struck me as an odd gesture but soon I realized the admiration these people had for this family.

Days turned into weeks and I continued returning to the bakery every day. I became fast friends with Hannah one of the waitresses on staff. I learned that six-year-old Mary helped prepare meals when she was not in school. I speak with Abraham when he came by my table. He often gave me his million dollar smile and a quick wave before he went into the kitchen. Sometimes he stopped and chatted with me for a moment, so today when he did I wasn't nervous or scared.

"Hello Annabelle, Have you written any new articles lately?"

"I've written a couple here and there but nothing concrete. Thank you for asking."

"I was wondering if you had any plans tomorrow. I'd like to take you on a picnic."

I noticed his cheeks turn red. Wow.

I sat there frozen in my chair for a moment. I cleared my throat before speaking.

"I'd love too," I responded shyly.

Wildflower

I didn't know what to expect from Abraham. I had never been on a date with an Amish young man before. I put the finishing touches on my make-up when I heard a horse trotting coming from down the road. I didn't want to seem eager so I left the screen door closed and sat on the couch to read a book. I opened the blinds up so I could see as he got closer. I felt the butterflies begin to swarm in my stomach as I watched the set of American Standardbred horses climb the final hill. I saw a green wagon trailing behind two horses. It was an open two-seater wagon, and even I knew that was more for romantic social calls.

The butterflies turned up a notch.

I stood and fixed a few strands of hair and checked my breath. I hadn't been on many dates in my life but I had a feeling this one was going to be life altering.

Abraham helped me into his wagon.

The seat was hard and moved when I moved. The swaying of the moving buggy caused me to grip the side. Eventually, I got used to the motion and my heart stilled. The brisk northern breeze cooled my flushed face as I took in the sights.

"Hey Abraham, how long does it take to make the bales of straw?"

"It takes one man many hours hacking the tall grass with a scythe," he said smiling. "But other farmers often pitch in and help one another. Some help even when they're unable to because they are gracious and kind individuals."

Abraham called those individuals God's disciples. I stared at this man in awe. I loved hearing him praise his community like he did because whether he knew it or not he was one of those disciples. His story reminded me of the weeks I sat at the bakery and watched the Hochstetlers as they prepared each dish with joy and hard work. I realized then that the Hochstetlers were also disciples of God. I took a deep breath in enjoying the smell of freshly cut straw mixed with Abraham's scent. He seemed to notice my hearty attempt at enjoying the scent of the countryside.

"The fresh air is nice, right?" Abraham drew in a deep breath.

"Have you worked at the dairy farm you were telling me about?" I asked curiously.

"No I haven't, I will start back again tomorrow so I won't see you again until the weekend. I only work in the bakery when work isn't available elsewhere."

A few moments later we pulled into a meadow filled with Eastern Daisies, Bearded Beggar sticks, swamp lilies, Bulbous Buttercups and Black-Eye Susans. It was full of colors. I saw reds and greens with bursts of yellow and blues. In the center of the white Elderberry and Meadow Rue sat a colorful quilt with a hand woven picnic basket on top. I looked around and saw grasshoppers jumping around and blue and yellow butterflies danced through the sky. Blue birds sat on branches twittering about.

"Oh Abraham, this is all so beautiful."

"I'm glad you like it. I wanted to find a place where I could get to know you."

I laced our hands together and we walked towards the quilt. I brushed my hands along the flowers. I stopped to smell a few; I fell down when a lady bug tickled my nose. I stayed there in that spot and looked up at the sky. What was I doing? I was busy falling in love and I forgot about my mission to find Ruth Hershberger. For now, I was going to enjoy this but I needed to use the weekdays to find out how to get in touch with Ruth.

I stood up and I continued to look around. I took everything in because I wanted to remember this day for the rest of my life. I saw his green buggy on the hillside, the cedar, and the pine trees swaying in the distance. I saw butterflies and dragonflies dancing through the sky. I watched the grasshoppers jump from flower the flower. A laugh escaped my mouth as I twirled around like a child. I felt like I had the world at the tip of my fingers.

And then there was Abraham.

He talked. I talked. He listened, paying full attention when I spoke. He never strayed from our conversations and he never looked bored.

The way he looked at me made me feel speial in a way I had never felt before.

I walked over to the quilt and sat beside Abraham. Together we talked about our hopes and dreams.

"Are you happy where you are in life?" I asked him. "Because I feel really lost."

"I was lost for some time but I prayed that one day I would figure out what I wanted and I found it. I want to open my own furniture store. Why do you feel lost?"

I got emotional. I don't know why. I felt the moisture build in my eyes for the first time since...I don't know when.

"I came to Sugar Grove in search of a woman. I'm trying to locate an Amish woman named Ruth Hershberger. I have some urgent information I need to discuss with her. She may be the woman who gave birth to me."

Abraham pulled me into his arms and I melted into his warm embrace.

"I promise that I'll help you in any way that I can," he whispered.

Abraham and I watched the sunset together. Our fingers danced together on the quilt. There were moments of silence but they were filled with laughter. Abraham always knew when my mind began wandering. He always attempted to pull me back and I was thankful for the distraction. I saw the stars form in the sky and knew our night was drawing to an end.

"Do you write books, *liebchen*?" Abraham asked.

"I haven't thought writing books lately but it was a dream of mine growing up. What does *liebchen* mean?"

"Sorry," he blushed I couldn't help it."

"What does it mean?"

"It means 'my love.'"

"Liebchen sounds better than my love if you ask me."

I learned he wanted to work with animals and wished one day to be a veterinarian. The money wasn't there so he wasn't sure how he could pull it off.

He looked at the sky and announced it was time to start heading home. The buggy ride home was silent but in a good way. I could see fireflies lighting up the sky and could hear crickets chirping in the night. This night felt too good to be true. It felt absolutely bewitching. When they made it to her cottage we heard an owl hooting nearby.

"I never heard such a noise in person," I laughed. I was used to horns honking, sirens blaring, and the usual city noises. I started to enjoy looking up and seeing the constellations in the sky and hearing the animals and insects talk in the night. It felt like a whole other universe out here. A universe I either never noticed or forgot about.

Abraham pulled up to the little yellow cottage on Danbury Lane and walked me to the door. He looked a little nervous before he finally spoke up.

"Would you like to attend Sunday Worship with my family? It is always nice to listen to the bishop tell tales about *Herr Gott*."

"Yes, I would love to join your family on Sunday."

"Perhaps you will see Ruth there."

"Perhaps I will."

Kiss Me

The week was long and brutal. I continued going to the bakery even though I knew Abraham wouldn't be there. I was glad Abraham wasn't here because could focus on finding Ruth. I looked through the local phone book and found a Hershberger family that lived in Sugar Grove. Their address was close by but I could feel myself cowering down. I also didn't want to march up to Ruth and say "Hi, I'm your daughter."

I learned enough to know that the Amish were close knit and they weren't keen on outsiders meddling in their business.

I woke up early Sunday morning and took a bubble bath. I was daydreaming about spending the day with the Hochstetlers and learning about the Amish community

I heard a knock on the door and put on my robe before I heard my name being called.

"Annabelle, are you in there?" said a deep male voice.

I recognized that voice but I wasn't dressed to meet him at the door. I stood behind the closed door and answered back.

"Abraham is that you?"

The last time I looked at the clock it had been six a.m. Who would be here so early?

"Yes, it is Abraham are you alright?" He sounded scared.

"I just got out of the shower, I'm going to unlock the doors and go back to my room. Count to sixty and then you can come in."

Abraham busted out laughing and then I heard his faint counting. I ran to the back of the cottage and slammed the door closed. I grabbed my dress off of the hanger and threw it over top of me. I started pulling curlers from my hair when I heard water running in the kitchen. I was curious about that but opted to put on my shoes and fix my hair instead.

Abraham helped me into the buggy. We trotted the three miles to his family farm and picked up his sisters Hannah and Mary. The girls looked a little flustered but neither said a word at first. Hannah broke the silence.

"Grosseldre and Maemm rode with Daed to the Yoder bauereie."

Mary apologized when she interrupted her sister but she saw Annabelle's uncomfortable shifting.

"Hannah, our guest doesn't speak Pennsylvania Dutch perhaps you should use Englisch."

Hannah's faced reddened before she apologized.

"Our grandparents rode with our parents to the Yoder Farm so we don't need to pick them up this morning."

"Mary, that was kind of you to include Annabelle into the conversation, *Herr Gott* is smiling down on you for your acts of kindness."

The buggy pulled onto a large farm and parked next to the other rows of wagons. The farm was beautifully maintained. There are usually animals roaming about but today they were confined to the barn. Worship was held on that warm summer morning because there were two hundred people that showed up to hear the bishop speak.

After he finished, children began playing a game in a nearby field. Men helped with farm work as the women prepared the covered dishes.

I took a tour of the farm then walked back to the others. Then I saw a woman who looked vaguely familiar. She was helping a small child fix his clothes near the outhouse. I waited until the child ran off before trying to speak with the woman. Maybe she knew Ruth or perhaps she is Ruth. There was something that was pulling me in the direction of that woman. I was about to greet her but she took one look at me, turned and walked away.

I felt as if I were punched in the stomach.

I felt couldn't breathe, I looked for the only one who knew my secret.

"Abraham, I am so sorry, but do you think you could take me home? I'm not feeling well."

"I need to let my parents know but I'll meet you at the buggy."

The next day, Abraham stopped by and asked if I wanted to take a walk.

He led me down a dirt road before we hit a walking trail. Then he took my hand before speaking.

We walked and talked for a while before Abraham spotted a stream. He found a large leaf and made a bowl out of it so that we could enjoy the water. We were walking again this time he took her with confidence and kissed it. We walked for a long time before I asked,

"Are we walking to my home in LA?"

"Come we will rest before we head back to your house," Abraham laughed.

He was used to long hours of walking but he understood that she wasn't accustomed to it.

"What happened today at the Yoder farm?"

"I tried to speak to this woman who looked familiar, but she ran away."

He said nothing, leading me to a hay field were we sat and rested.

I pulled a piece of straw lose and gathered the courage to see where this relationship was going.

"Have you ever been in love?" I asked timidly.

Abraham smiled like he was just pondering the topic himself.

"Yes, I have been in love," he smiled. "This woman brightens the sky when she steps into the sunlight. She lights up a room when she walks in with a smile on her face. I hear her heart beats and my world feels absolute. She walks barefoot in the sand and has skin the color of ivory. Her eyes are the color of storm clouds on a hot summer's day. Her lips look like ripe cherries ready for tasting."

He leaned over and caressed my cheek.

I didn't know what to say.

"Annabelle Michaels, I love you more than I ever thought possible. I'd rather die a lonely man before I'd ever give you up."

"I don't know what to say."

"We had better start back before it gets too late," he said. "I have to work in the morning and you need to find Ruth."

Deception

The next morning I woke up feeling fresh and determined. I decided to take matters into my own hands. I decided to go to the Hershberger farm and meet this family. I pulled out a cookbook from the cabinet. I decided to make a chicken casserole to show respect for their family. It took me a few hours to get things together and it was almost lunch time. I loaded the rental car and drove to the address I found the other day.

I pulled up to the farm and knocked on the door. The paint was peeling from the wood and the hinges were rusted. There was a large run-down barn behind the house and there was a fenced off area on one side of the house. I knocked again and shouted a greeting. An elderly woman came to the door; she spoke little English and told me to go around back.

I walked over to the fenced area.

"Hello, is anyone here?"

I heard the woman talking to a man in hushed tones but the man turned and walked away, but not before I could see tension rise in his shoulders.

I took a deep breath and she walked up to the woman I saw the other day.

"Good afternoon, I am Annabelle Michaels and I work with the LA Times. I'd like to write a story on your dairy farm if that is ok with you. We want to determine if there is a large difference in the way milk is produced."

The woman chuckled before responding

"I know you came here because you want to know if you're my boppli. I know you want to know if I am your Maemm."

Before I could answer I saw someone coming toward me out of the corner of my eye.

Abraham.

I couldn't believe it Abraham knew Ruth all along. I had to know why he didn't tell me but right now I just wanted him to know that I now know his secret.

I walked over to him and asked to speak with him alone. He said he needed to finish his shift and he would come to the cottage so we could talk.

I drove the three miles back to the cottage in tears, I had learned who Ruth was, and I learned Abraham was manipulative and he kept things from those he loved. Neither obviously loved me or cared for me or they would have been honest from the start.

I curled up on the couch waiting to hear from the airlines. I was booking a ticket and getting out of this small town.

Then I heard a feint knock at the door. I opened the door and there standing was not Abraham but Ruth; my birth mother was standing right in her doorway. It was the one thing I always wanted and often dreamed of. I didn't care if I had the perfect man or the comfiest shoes. I just wanted to be accepted by the woman who gave up on me.

I invited Ruth in and listened to her tale that began twenty-three years ago. I learned my dad was a fisherman and my parents met when my dad delivered fish to the local market. He would often purchase jam from her mom's fruit stand and one time he bought all her jam. He stopped by each summer for three years before her mom finally grew the courage to leave her roots and locate the man that filled her soul. My mother found my father and she claimed he was the love of her life but she only had a few short months with him. She felt punished by God when they discovered he had colon cancer. Her mom had just discovered she was pregnant with me when her father told her the news. My father stayed with my mom for the first two months but when he died my mother was forced to live in a women's shelter until she gave birth. She put me up for adoption and when I was adopted Ruth moved back to her parents and joined the Amish community.

Ruth admitted that she never mentioned me until Abraham confronted her a few weeks ago. Ruth learned I was getting impatient and wanted to meet her but Ruth was ashamed that she hid her secret for so long. That was when Ruth told her story to the community and to her husband. He knew of her relationship with my father but he was unaware she conceived a child. I drew in a deep breath and immediately thought of Abraham.

There was a knock on the door and we both knew who it was. I opened the door and ushered him to the swing that faced the hills.

"Abraham, how long have you known about her being my mom?"

His shoulders sank then he fell to his knees. I saw tears escape his eyes, but there was no way I was going to let him get away that easily. No matter how much I loved this man, he kept something from important from the person he swore he loved.

"*Liebchen*, I realized the day that you mentioned your birth mother's name. I won't lie, I knew who she was, but I wanted to make sure it was the right person. I didn't want to accuse someone of something she never did. Once I discovered she was the woman you were searching for I asked her to come to you when she was ready because it's her news to share. I wasn't around then and I don't know much now. I do know that there is much she eager to tell and in time I'm sure she will. We both care deeply about you and are worried you will leave. I'm sorry I kept any information from you, I only did it out of protection."

I looked into his eyes as he faced me and I saw the same passion as when he told me about God's disciples. He was helping a friend in need. This friend just happened to be my mother.

I hadn't seen real feeling until I saw this man's face. It was full of emotions, guilt mixed with grief and a face stained with tears. He held onto my leg like it was the only thing holding us together. I could turn cold and run away but instead, I dropped to my knees and placed my head on his chest. All I wanted was Abraham and Ruth in my life. I looked up and I kissed him hard. I fell into his arms and confessed.

"Abraham Thomas Hochstetler, *Ich liebe dich,* than one could love one's self."

I used the Dutch phrase for I love you trying to prove my devotion to his heritage.

"I think of you daily and I pray for your safety each night. I hold you in my heart where I've held no other. There is no way I would turn and walk away. I want to be a part of your life."

He got down on one knee and took my hand in his.

"Annabelle Naomi Michaels Hershberger, will you marry me?"

AMISH SUNSET

NANCY MANN

Chapter I

Rain decorated the grassy fields of Lancaster County. The sky was a cloud grey, the sun remaining absent as the county mourned for the loss of William Bradshire, a carpenter that had been known throughout the county for his kindness and love towards the people around him.

Friends and family had gathered in the county's cemetery for William's funeral, one of the mourners being William's love, Mary Lee Warner. Out of everyone there, Mary was the most damaged from it. William's parents had passed on early in his life due to illnesses and the remaining family he had weren't as close. If anything, Mary was the only one there who truly was family to him.

As Bishop David spoke about his memories with William, Mary thought to herself how God could do such a thing, to take away an innocent being this early in his life. William was only in his mid-twenties, like Mary. He had so much to experience in his life, but it was stripped away from him so early due to the accident.

"If anyone has anything to say, speak now." Bishop David said, stepping back and letting anyone step forward to speak.

There was a long pause, silence being present as Mary thought to herself. Eventually, she took a step forward, standing in front of the casket as she let out a depressed sigh.

"William...had a beautiful soul," Mary said quietly, holding onto a wildflower, "a soul that I have yet to find in any other human being."

Everyone was watching her speak, seeing what Mary had in her hand and what she had to say about William being gone.

"I can't imagine not meeting him in my life...all the memories we've made together...all the laughter, the love...I'm going to miss it." Mary spoke as tears ran down her cheeks. "I don't know if I will find another William in my life."

Some of William's family members began to have tears fall too as they listened to Mary's words about their lost kin. Mary soon stepped back from the casket, having finished speaking on the behalf of William's death. Bishop David soon stepped forward again, wiping some tears from his own eyes.

"Thank you Mary...I will say, before I close in prayer, that it will be difficult to find another William in our lives." Bishop David said to Mary before opening his Bible.

Verses from the Bible were soon spoken out loud, everybody bowing their heads in prayer as Bishop David spoke. While everyone listened, Mary wasn't listening to the verses, in fact, she was in her own mind at this point.

"Why God...why would you take William away from me?" Mary thought to herself. *"William didn't even get half way into his life...why would you take him now?"*

As she struggled with the idea of William passing on, Bishop David finished reading the verses, quietly speaking the word *amen* as he closed his Bible, everybody soon leaving the scene of the funeral, letting the casket to be lowered into the grave. While the casket lowered, Mary was the only one present, witnessing her love's final presence on the surface of Earth.

In regards to funeral traditions of the Amish, flowers were not placed on the casket. For Mary though, traditions meant nothing to her in this occasion. She took the wildflower that she was holding in her hand and tossed it down into the undug grave, letting it land on the coffin before the gravediggers began to bury the coffin.

"I love you so much William." Mary said as the coffin soon disappeared from the soil piling on top. Tears continued to fall onto the soil as she left the site of the funeral.

Chapter II

Several years later...the county had returned back to its normal ways, except for Mary. Ever since William passed away, Mary wasn't her old self. Her old cheerful personality had passed on as well, leaving her a closed up, emotionless woman in her mid-twenties.

She tried to return back to a normal life by going to church, seeing if God might be able to help her find peace, but the more she went the church, the more she began to question God. At times, she would find herself being angry at God for taking William away this early in his life. Eventually, Mary stopped going to church, which brought the concern of Bishop David, leading him to go to Mary's home.

Her house was a little way from town, being near one of the farms. She lived in a large house that belonged to William and his parents. Now that William passed on, Mary now owned the house and lived in it by herself.

Bishop David knocked on the front door, waiting for it to be opened. It took a few knocks before the door finally opened, Mary standing there in a stone grey dress.

"Yes?" Mary quietly said, looking at him with her expressionless face.

"May I come in?" Bishop David asked softly, his expression being hopeful that she would accept his request.

Mary let out a quiet sigh before she nodded, stepping out of the way for Bishop David to come in.

"Thank you...Mary." He said, soon walking into her home, looking around.

Mary shut the door behind Bishop David, walking past him and sitting down on a chair in the living room, continuing what she was doing before he knocked. When Bishop David sat down across from her, he noticed that she was knitting a quilt.

"Oh...I see that you've been busy with making a quilt." Bishop David said, giving Mary a gentle smile.

"Quilts. I've been busy making quilts." She said quickly, pointing in the corner to a basket of several quilts.

Bishop David was surprised by the amount of quilts she had made. "That's quite the number of quilts Mary." He said with a small laugh after.

Mary raised her eyebrows as she continued to knit the quilt. "I've found that work is one of the few things that keeps me from thinking about the past." She said softly, not making eye contact with Bishop David.

"Oh...well...if that's what helps you find peace." He said quietly, rubbing the back of his neck before he finally decided to talk about why he wanted to talk to her. "Mary...I'm worried about you."

She heard Bishop David, stopping for a second before she continued knitting the quilt. "Why?" Mary questioned him.

"I'm concerned for you because you haven't been going to church for months." Bishop David finally said, looking at her with a worried expression. "You were always an avid church-goer when William..." He said before realizing what he said, stopping in mid-sentence.

Mary immediately looked up when Bishop David brought up William, her knitting ceasing before she let out a sigh of disbelief escape her lips. She set the quilt and knitting needle down. "Please, do not ever bring up William to me again when comparing me to then and now." Mary said, her voice trembling as she had grown an upset expression.

Bishop David had become silent as he listened to Mary finally speak to him.

"I'm no longer the Mary from then because of the events that happened, and if you want to visit me and tell me how I use to love church and that you're concerned with me not being there on Sundays, then don't even speak, you're wasting your breath." Mary said to him, her eyes staring into his intensely.

Bishop David heard everything she was saying before he let out a sigh of sympathy. "I'm sorry Mary that you're like this...I didn't come here today to chastise you about not attending church. I came here because I'm really concerned for what you've become. I want happiness for you, I want you to have that cheerful personality that everybody knew you for." He said softly, standing up from sitting, looking down at her. "Always remember Mary, we all face events in life that we don't want, but it's all a part of God's plan for something greater."

Mary just glared at him the whole time he spoke, not even acknowledging the things he said. "I would like you to leave."

Bishop David heard her request and nodded softly, walking away from where they were at and leaving the house.

She had watched him leave through the windows before she finally reached for her knitting needles and quilt, continuing to knit as she thought about what he said about God having a plan for everyone. To her, God's plan was killing William and taking away something that she loved most in the world, when she didn't have anyone else.

"Forget God." Mary said to herself quietly, having completely lost faith and love in God.

Chapter III

One stormy night soon had arrived in Lancaster County. Rain had arrived over the town and fields, the sound of sharp pellets hitting the roofs and windows of each building. The window whirled between each building, the sounds of wind wailing could be heard by anyone who was awake.

While the storm stayed present in the county, Mary was asleep in her bed, although she wasn't sleeping soundly. The red-headed woman was having a nightmare, causing her to toss back and forth in her sleep before some sort of sound interrupted her slumber.

KNOCK KNOCK KNOCK

Mary sat right up from her bed like a vampire in a coffin, rubbing her eyes. "What on Earth?" She said to herself, looking around the room as she wondered what caused her to wake up.

KNOCK KNOCK KNOCK

This time, the red-head heard the solution to the noise. "Who could be at my door in the middle of the night?" Mary got out of her bed, wrapping her blanket around herself to cover her nightgown. She made her way down the stairs of her home before seeing the front door. Once she got to the door, she slowly opened it, seeing who it was.

There was a man, about her age, with a young daughter about six-years-old. They were wet from head to toe, shivering as they looked at Mary.

"Please...do you have room in your home for my child and I? We come from far away to Lancaster County...we have no home, no food." The man said, his tone being a desperate one.

Mary had no idea that this was what waited for her on the other side of the door. "I...Well..." She looked at the two before she finally nodded quickly, stepping out of the way.

"Oh thank you...thank you!" The man said happily and emotionally. He quickly moved inside, Mary shutting the door behind the two. Even though they were inside, away from the rain, they still were shivering in the dark home. Mary saw how cold they were and immediately knew what they needed.

She quickly went over to the fireplace in the living room, taking two logs that were on the side of the hearth in a pile and putting them inside the fireplace. After a few attempts of trying to get a fire started, she eventually managed to do so, an orange glow illuminating the living room.

Once the man saw the fire, he moved his daughter close to the fireplace, trying to get her as warm as possible. Mary saw what he was trying to do and quickly went over to the eight-year-old, wrapping her blanket around the child. The man soon began to dry off her daughter while at the same time trying to get her warm.

"There you go...nice and warm now. Away from the cold rain." He said quietly to his daughter, holding her close as he sat in front of the fireplace with her.

The daughter shivered still, but the warmth from the fire and the blanket caused the shivering to decrease as the time went by.

Mary stood behind the two, watching them and making sure that they were okay. "Are you warm enough?" She asked them, having held one of the quilts she had made in her hands to give to the man.

"Yes...thank you kind miss." He said quietly, holding his daughter close before taking the quilt from Mary, wrapping it around himself.

With the two warming themselves up from the fire, Mary decided to grab another quilt for herself before sitting down on her couch. She wrapped the quilt around her body so she could be warm too. Since she now had two "guests" in her home, she didn't want to go upstairs, back to bed, with the knowledge that two strangers were downstairs in her home, two people who she had no idea who they were.

"Maybe they're thieves," Mary thought to herself, studying the two strangers. *"Although...she looks pretty young to be a thief."* She finally decided to speak up, wanting to figure out who they were. "Where did you two come from?"

The man looked back at her, hearing her question before he began to reply to her. "We came from Somerset County." The man answered, still trying to warm up his daughter.

"Oh...that's far from here." Mary replied, sitting down on her couch, looking at the man.

"It very much is..." The man nodded, looking at her. "Do you know if there's any housing here in Lancaster County?"

Mary heard her question before she shrugged. "I'm not too sure. Are you looking for a place to stay?"

The man nodded, looking down at his daughter. She had fallen into slumber and had a warm expression on her face and had stopped shivering, indicating she was no longer freezing. "Yes."

She heard him and asked some more questions in order to get to know him. "Why Lancaster County? I'm sure there's plenty of other settlements along the way."

"I just," The man began to say, rubbing the back of his neck nervously, "I don't know...I guess I've heard a lot of great things about Lancaster. Figured that it would be a great place for my daughter to grow up in."

Mary nodded when he stated that it'd be a good place for his daughter to grow up in. "Lancaster really is a nice place to grow up in...a good place to start a fam-" she began to say before stopping when she was about to say "family." It reminded her of what she has always wanted to have and that made her think of William and her. "Well, it's a good place to meet nice and caring people."

The man saw her reaction when she was talking about family, but decided not to question it in order to remain polite. "That's good to hear...by the way," the man began to say, looking at her once again, "what is your name?"

She heard him and replied softly. "Mary...my name is Mary Lee Warner."

When the man heard her, he smiled softly. "That's a beautiful name."

Mary smiled softly when he complimented her name. "What about you? What's your name?"

"Robert." He said quietly, before looking down at his daughter, gently stroking her hair. "The little one is Miriam."

Chapter IV

The next morning had arrived, the rain was now gone, the only trace of rain being the puddles in the dirt. Mary decided to help Robert and Miriam out by going down to the church to see Bishop David could help them out.

Entering the church, there were only a few people present in the pews, praying to the Lord about whatever comes to their attention. Bishop David was not preaching, considering it was a Tuesday, so chances were he was at his home.

"Doesn't look like he's here." Mary said, turning around and leading Robert and Miriam out.

"Who are we looking for exactly?" Robert said, holding his daughter's hand as they walked towards Bishop David's house.

"We're looking for David, Lancaster County's bishop. He might be able to help you out with moving here." Mary replied, reaching the bishop's house before knocking on the door. Not too long after the knock, the door opened, Bishop David standing there.

"Mary?" He said, a little surprised. "What brings you here today?"

Mary explained the whole story to him, telling the bishop that Robert and Miriam showed up in the middle of the night, needing a place to stay and that they wanted to move to Lancaster.

"I see..." Bishop David said quietly, scratching his beard as he thought about it. "Unfortunately, there isn't any houses available right now."

Mary heard the news and let out a quiet groan. "So where will they stay if they don't have a home?"

Bishop David heard her before looking at the two, looking at Mary again. "Can I talk to you privately Mary?"

Mary was confused as to why, but nodded as she stepped inside the bishop's house. "What did you want to talk to me about?"

Bishop David looked at her before he let out a quiet sigh. "I wanted to talk to you privately about where they're going to stay. I believe they should continue living at your house until a new house can be built here in the county."

She listened to what he said before hearing his statement about the two staying at her home. "What? No. I can't have people living at my house."

Bishop David gave her a confused look. "Why not? You have one of the biggest houses here in Lancaster County. You're not living with anyone. There's plenty of room in the house for someone."

"Because, I don't have enough food to feed two more people. I don't want to start housing people." Mary was quick to say, folding her arms. "I can't let strangers come into my home and make themselves acquainted to the hou-"

"Mary." Bishop David interrupted, clearly showing he was getting irritated with her. "Enough with the excuses. I'm not going to force you to let them in. I'm only suggesting you give the two of them a home. It's not permanent, but where else are they going to go?" He asked Mary, looking at her with a serious expression. "They can't move into anyone else's home. They all have families, rather large ones too."

She listened to him, looking into his eyes as she thought about everything he was saying. Bishop David was right in many ways. Most families in the county had large families, homes that were already crowded. With Mary's house, it was just her. He even said that it wasn't permanent, so it'd be something that Mary didn't have to deal with for too long.

"I guess...I could have them stay for a little while." Mary finally admitted, realizing that she could be a little generous.

"Thank you Mary." Bishop David said before leading her back outside, now facing Robert. "We will discuss adding a house whenever I meet my colleagues. Until we can get a house added to the county, you'll have to stay with Mary for the time being."

Robert listened to what Bishop David said, nodding softly. "Okay, thank you."

Bishop David smiled softly, heading back into the house before closing the door.

Robert and Miriam turned toward Mary, looking at her. "So...are we going to back to the nice lady's house?" Miriam asked her father.

Mary heard her and couldn't help but smile. "Yes…yes you are."

Robert watched the two interact before he couldn't help but smile, seeing this stranger being so nice to his daughter.

"Alright. Let's head back to the house so I can get a room prepped up for you two." Mary said, clapping her hands together when she knew what she needed to do.

Chapter V

A couple of months passed by in Mary's household. The two strangers that had showed up on her doorstep were now friends of hers, having brightened up the household little by little. As Mary got to know Robert, he started feeling more and more comfortable around him, the two even joking around with each other.

With Miriam, she started to look up towards Mary as a mother figure, every now and then the little girl called Mary mom. Mary would hear this and laugh, finding it humorous that Robert's daughter called her mom.

While everyone was getting along just fine, Mary started to remember William again, every time she looked at Robert. There was something about Robert that reminded her of William. It might've been the way he made her laugh or the way he showed kindness to people. Whatever it was, Mary could see William through Robert, which made her think about if she found another William in her life.

It was now 6 PM and Robert and Miriam had finished eating dinner with Mary. When they finished, Robert decided to take Miriam to bed, since she started dozing off during dinner. Once she was in bed, she was out cold.

"She must've been really tired today. Miriam never goes to bed this early." Robert said, walking back into the kitchen. "I don't blame her...she didn't sleep that well last night."

"Oh poor thing." Mary said, cleaning the dishes in the sink. "I hope she rests well tonight."

"She probably will." Robert said, walking over before leaning against the counter. "So...what do you want to do?"

Mary continued to wash the dishes before she stopped, soon looking at him. "What do you mean?"

"Well I mean...Miriam is in bed early. Do you want to go out for a walk?" Robert replied, looking at her and waiting to hear an answer.

She looked at him before looking down at the dishes, thinking about his offer before setting the plates down. "I would enjoy that."

He smiled brightly before he walked out of the kitchen, planning on getting his jacket.

It didn't take long before the two were on an adventure, walking around the county in the early evening. The sky was an vibrant orange, the sun easing itself behind the hills.

"Wow...that's a beautiful sunset." Robert said softly, looking at it.

"It sure is." Mary said quietly, looking at it before she looked at Robert. With the two of them having grown closer, she soon started to think more in regards of making their relationship a bit more than friends. "Can I show you something?"

Robert heard her, turning his head and looking at her before he smiled softly. "Yeah of course."

Mary smiled brightly before leading him into the woods, walking in a certain direction. As for Robert, he wasn't sure where she was taking him, which made him a little nervous. Eventually, the two arrived in a rather large open area in the woods, a grass area that was decorated with wildflowers.

"Wow..." Robert quietly said to himself, stepping forward and starting to walk towards the flowers. "They're beautiful."

Mary stood behind Robert, watching his response before walking with him again. "I know. I love coming to this place. It reminds me of so many happy memories." She said before she began to lay down in the grass, looking at the sky that had become as orange as a Doris Longwing Butterfly's wing.

Robert watched what she did before he followed her actions, lying next to her as the two watched the sky. "You have quite the spot...especially one that you value." He smiled softly, relaxing on the grass.

The two watched the sky for a few, enjoying the time to relax with each other. Eventually, Robert spoke up, a question that had been resonating within him.

"How come you didn't want to let us live with you a few months ago?" He quietly said, still looking at the sky, some clouds gently moving along in the sky.

Mary heard him and gave him a confused look. "What do you mean?"

"You were talking to Bishop David the morning after the rainstorm. You told him that you didn't want anyone staying at the house because you didn't have enough food and didn't want housing people. Part of me though doesn't believe that."

Mary listened to what Robert was saying, her expression staying confused before her expression became more of a look of hesitant.

"There's something more than not enough food and not wanting to house people huh? You don't have to tell me, but just know I'm here if you want to talk." Robert said quietly, wanting to assure that she could trust him.

She listened to what he said before she began biting her own lip, thinking to herself before she let out a quiet sigh. "There is...there's a lot more to it. I think it's fair that you should know."

He heard her response to his question and turned onto his side, looking at her now as she began to speak about what the reason for not wanting anyone to live with her.

"It all has to do with a man I loved...a man named William." Mary said quietly.

Chapter VI

William Bradshire...a carpenter of Lancaster County. Most of the county knew him as the kind man who cared about everyone around him, even the ones who didn't care for him. William was the prime example of what it means to follow Christ's footsteps. He showed a strong love towards God, helped out around his community, showed love towards everyone, taught the youth about the Bible, and that's just the peak of the iceberg.

Sometimes in life though, bad things can occur that change one's life. For William, it was losing his parents at the age of eighteen. With his parents gone, he now owned the house, but that meant nothing to William. For a long time, he had struggled with the fact that his parents were gone, but during this time, he still continued to help people, having put them first before himself.

A great example of William putting others first was one cold, dark night. There was a knock on his door, the knock having echoed the entire silent household. When William opened his front door, he found a shivering girl his age, looking up at him. This girl was Mary.

The young girl had ran away from home, angry at her parents and her peers around her community. She was looking for a place to stay, which was she ended up on William's doorstep, a stranger to him. William was caring enough to immediately let her in; he even allowed her to stay as long as she needed. Even though she could've left any time, she found herself a priceless friendship.

Eventually, as time progressed, the redhead soon fell in love with William, the same happening with the boy. The two ended up revealing their love for each other when they discovered and rested in the grass area in the woods with the wildflowers. Ever since then, they were two peas in a pod.

As time progressed, they became closer and closer, almost being one soul. Mary began helping out in the community with him while developing a strong love of God since William introduced her to Him. Eventually, William decided that he was going to ask Mary for her hand in marriage, but his colleagues asked for his help in finishing the construction of a barn.

Unfortunately, William never had the chance to pop the question due to the accident. While he was watching his colleagues raise one of the barn walls up by pulling it up with ropes, the ropes snapped and the wall soon fell on William, his chances of escaping the wall very low with how fast the whole situation took. Sadly, William didn't survive the heavy barn wall crushing him.

Word soon got out around the county about William dying from the accident, which Mary soon heard about. She was devastated, crushed, her heart torn into pieces for the loss of her one true love.

After William had passed, Mary was given the house, considering she basically lived there and was a member of the community. During this time, Mary closed herself off from the rest of the world, locking herself away in her home, mourning the loss of William. She even decided to not let anyone into the house after the loss in order to keep the house peaceful, like it was when William and her were in it.

Even in the present, Mary still has nightmares about the whole incident, nightmares that remind her of the loss of William.

"If only I were there to stop him...to get him out of the way...If only I were there...he'd still be alive."

Chapter VII

Once Mary finished telling Robert the story, she had developed some tears from the memory of William's death.

"Now you know why I don't let anyone into the house...I know...it sounds insane, for the girlfriend of someone who has departed to keep the house like a temple. You must think I'm crazy..." Mary said quietly, wiping her tears.

"Oh no..." Robert said, looking at her. "I don't think you're insane at all...I can see why you value the house so much. All the memories with William...the laughter...the peace...everything about it...you don't want anyone to ruin this place for you." He said softly, gently resting his hand on hers. "I'm sorry...I didn't know this was the reason why you didn't want us here."

Mary heard him and finally broke down, tears rolling down her cheeks as she covered her face with her hands, muffled crying heard behind it. Robert reached for her and wrapped his arms around her, holding her close as he embraced her.

"Shhh...it's okay...Mary." Robert quietly said, stroking her hair gently to calm her down. "It's okay..."

After years of suppressing the memories of William and her, the pain she has endured from remembering his death, the many tears she had held back, she finally broke down and let her tears flow.

"I miss him so much...every day I wish I could see him again...tell him that I wish I could've saved him from the wall...I wish I could've done something." She said, pressing her face against Robert's shoulder as she shook from her crying.

"You couldn't do anything Mary...you had no idea that would happen..." Robert said softly, continuing to hold her close as she cried against him. "Look on the bright side...with William having a strong love for God, he's finally in Heaven where he can be with God...walk along with him...talk to him...laugh with him."

With Robert's words entering Mary's ears, it made her cry more. He was right in the sense that she wouldn't have known and that he's in a better place now. Her heart ached as she recalled all the memories of William from when they met to his death. All the memories were mainly happy and ones that would make her laugh whenever she looked back to them. Even though William was gone, she remembered one thing...William lives on through her. The memories, the house, the ideology, everything that William was made up of lives on through Mary. With this thought, she felt like she could finally get over the tragedy of losing William and achieve peace.

"Thank you...Robert...Thank you." Mary said quietly, looking up at him with tears in her eyes.

Robert looked down at her, confused as to why she was telling him thank you. "For what?" He laughed gently, wiping the tears away from her eyes.

"For saying all of those things about William and I...I've spent all these years holding onto William's tragedy and blaming myself for not being able to help him, but now I can finally find peace and let go of the tragedy...thank you...Robert." She finally said, looking at him as she gently reached up, stroking his cheek before she finally decided to lean in, kissing him gently.

Robert was caught off guard with the kiss, his eyebrows raising as she held her in his arms. Eventually, she broke the kiss, resting her head on his should. "Let's go back home...it's getting late." Mary said quietly, her eyes now closed.

Even though Robert had thought about pushing their relationship to another level, there was something that was holding him from reaching that level, something that had followed him from his previous home.

Chapter VIII

Many weeks had passed by since Mary told Robert about her past. Mary was in a much brighter mood, slowly building herself up again by socializing with people, going to church again, which made Bishop David happy, and she started wearing colorful clothes again.

Robert was thinking about what Mary had done in the wildflower area in the woods on the porch. He wanted to moved towards the next step, but the past was catching up with him.

"Hey!" Mary called out, coming up to the house with Miriam. "We've got dinner!"

He snapped back into reality, smiling gently when he saw the two. "Oh...that's wonderful. Looks delicious." Robert said, standing up and helping them take the food inside the house.

"I decided to cook something special for you...to thank you for helping me return back to my old self again."

Robert smiled and chuckled nervously, rubbing the back of his neck. "Oh...you don't have to do that."

"But papa," Miriam spoke out, looking at him, "look at the food! It looks delicious! At least let mom...Mary cook it for me."

Both Robert and Mary laughed at Miriam's comment, Mary picking her up and holding her.

"Okay, well if Robert doesn't want his special dinner, then I'll cook it for you." She said, walking in with the child.

"That'd be fantastic!" Miriam exclaimed happily.

Robert followed behind the two with the groceries, his expression being lost in thought as he thought about the past.

Dinner time soon arrived, everyone now seated at the table as they waited for Mary to come in with the special dinner.

"Whatever she's cooking, it smells delicious." Miriam said, excited to eat.

In a matter of minutes, Mary came out with a cooked turkey, the skin being a golden crisp.

Even though Robert wasn't asking for a special dinner, he was impressed with how the turkey came out. "Wow, looks really good Mary."

She smiled brightly, setting the plate down. "Well I'm glad you like it so much. I've got more coming out. I cooked some corn, made so mashed potatoes, have some greens." Mary explained to them as she walked back into the kitchen.

It took a few trips for her before she finally could sit down at the table with the two. "Alright, dig in." Mary said, taking her knife and fork, cutting into the turkey and scooping up a little bit of everything.

The dinner that they had all together was nice. Lots of laughter, lots of compliments, complete joy filled the room between Miriam and Mary, although Robert was most of the time quiet. After dinner, Miriam decided to go play with her doll in the living room while Mary and Robert were in the kitchen, cleaning the dishes.

While they were in there, Robert remained quiet, lost in his thoughts as he kept trying to shake it off. It didn't take too long though for Mary to see something was bothering him.

"You've been awfully quiet this evening...is there something wrong?" Mary asked him, continuing to wash the dishes.

"No." Robert said vaguely, not wanting to get into what was bothering him.

"You sure?" She said softly, looking at him. "You seem like you're thinking really hard about something."

"Don't worry about it." Robert said to her, trying to avoid explaining his thoughts.

Eventually, Mary let out a quiet sigh before setting her dish down, turning toward Robert.

"You know if something is troubling you, you can te-" Mary began to say to him.

"Drop it." Robert said harshly, looking at her for a few quick seconds before he finally set his plate down, shaking his head. "Just forget it...I'm going to bed." He said, leaving the kitchen and walking upstairs.

Mary was shocked by the way Robert reacted, considering it wasn't normal for Robert to be this way.

Miriam heard the commotion from the living room, looking at Mary. "Is papa upset about something?" She said with a concerned voice.

Mary heard Miriam and shook her head. "Don't worry about it dear. He just needs some time to himself."

Chapter IX

Robert currently laid in Mary's bed upstairs, his eyes closed as he tried sleeping. He didn't mean to snap at Mary, but considering his thoughts were getting to him, it was bound to happen. As he attempted to sleep, he soon felt something lay next to him, which interrupted his slumber. He opened his eyes and turned to look and see if it was Mary.

Of course, he was right in this situation. Mary was in her nightgown, having crawled in bed with Robert, getting cozy. Once he saw it was Mary, he returned back to his previous position, his back facing her. Still trying to avoid breaking the news to Mary, he soon felt her arms around his stomach, her body soon pressing against his back.

"What's going on with you? You're usually not like this." She said softly, resting her head against his back.

"I don't know Mary...I don't know." Robert said quietly, his eyes still closed.

"I feel like you do know Robert." Mary finally said. "I just feel like you don't want to tell me what you're thinking of."

He heard what she said, but didn't reply to it. The only thing he did was sit in silence with his eyes closed, trying to fall into slumber.

"You know I'm here if you want to tell me what's bothering you. I think it'd be healthy if you did though because you won't get any sleep with you thinking about whatever you're thinking. I know from experience." Mary quietly said, now closing her eyes as she rested her head against his back.

Robert listened to what she was saying before he let out a quiet sigh, trying to think about how he would explain his thoughts to her. Eventually, he decided to be straightforward with her.

"You know why I decided to move to Lancaster County?" He asked Mary quietly.

She merely shook her head against his back, indicating that she didn't know why he moved here. "Aside from finding a new home, no I don't."

Robert listened to what she had to say before he continued. "I left my previous home because my wife walked out on Miriam and I."

When Mary heard this, her eyes opened up and she sat up, looking down at him. "What? That's horrible! Why would she do that?"

Once Mary sat up, Robert turned so that he was laying on his back, now looking up at her. "To be honest...maybe I married the wrong person. She just...everything seemed fine to me. She was a good mother, I was a good father, we lived a happy life, but then one day..." He said before stopping, thinking back to that day before telling Mary what happened.

———————————

"Sara?" He called out, looking around his home. "Where are you?

While he walked around the house, Miriam watched him, not understanding what was going on. "Papa? What's going on?"

"I can't find mom. She's gone." Robert said, his tone being a little more scared. "Maybe she left something saying where she went. Yeah...she leaves notes."

"Maybe...I'll help you try and find something" Miriam said, getting off of the couch before walking around their home, trying find anything that could lead to the mystery of where Robert's wife went.

Eventually, Miriam found a note that had fallen on the side of the bed. "Papa!" She called out. "I found a note!"

Robert immediately ran into the room, seeing the note in Miriam's hand. He took the note from her and began reading it. Although the hope he had on his expression when he found the note soon faded the more he continued to read it. In fact, he soon had become emotionless from what was written on the note.

"What does it say papa?" Miriam asked, looking up at him.

Robert finished reading the note, looking down at Miriam before folding the note in half, tucking it into his pocket. "Don't worry about it sweetheart. I think though...we need to move away from this county."

When Miriam heard this, she was completely confused. "Why? Why do we need to move?"

He heard her before he picked her up, looking around the house one last time. "Because I think we will find somewhere else that'll be better for the both of us."

"We basically left the county with nothing but the clothes on our back. I couldn't stand living in the same county as her and live in a house that we lived in together." Robert said quietly, looking at Mary as he finished explaining his story. "Would you stay in the same place if you found out your love left you and your child for someone else?"

When Mary heard this, she let out a depressed sigh. "No...I don't think I would." She said quietly. "Is that what's been on your mind today?"

Robert heard her before nodding softly. "I've been thinking about it for a long time now...I've wanted to move onto the next step in our relationship, but...I fear that something would happen again...I fear the odds of you walking out on us."

Once Robert said that, Mary spoke up in a more serious tone. "Robert...look at me."

Robert did as told and look into her eyes, seeing what she would say.

"I would never do that...ever in my life." Mary said, looking at him as she gently rested her hand on his cheek. "I wouldn't do something to hurt you and Miriam...I love you both, with all my heart." She said to him before she gently kissed him, breaking it soon after before resting her head on his chest. "You don't need to worry about me every walking out on you two...I care about you two so much that my heart aches. I wouldn't even think about walking out on you two."

When Robert heard this, he let out a relieved sigh, his arms wrapping around her and hugging her against him. "I love you so much Mary..."

"I love you too Robert..."

THE END

AMISH AMITY

TRACY BOSWELL

Chapter 1

Rain just kept falling, never ending without any intention to stop, large puddles had gathered on the muddy grounds around the big barn, and water gushed down the eroded embankment running alongside the road, causing the road to be completely flooded. But no amount of rain would prevent Amity, Betty and Rachel to do what they came here to do. Having been friends since childhood, the three women were inseparable. Neither of them were married or promised to anyone yet, and although they are well beyond the age most girls in their community starts to settle down to start a family, it never really bothered them.

Amity was strong willed and mouthy young woman, who voiced her opinion whenever she felt it mattered. Of course her father, Bishop Gunther didn't quite approve of her behaviour at times, but he did support her willingness to stand up for herself. Bishop Gunther on the other hand wasn't like most others in their faith; he was more lenient and accepting than most, always promoting change within reason. He insisted that households started using gas stoves instead of coal stoves. He had even arranged to buy a truck to help the community to cart goods to the local market in town. According to him, modern change to a bare minimum does not give the devil a foothold, it just shows the devil that they are capable of change without modern ways ruling their lives and changing who they are or distracting them from things that matter most.

Betty, much like Amity also had a strong personality, one she definitely got from her mother, but she also had a mischievous streak. When the elders instructed the children not to play in the rain, she was always the first to splash in muddy puddles. When they had their social events, she was the one who would pull pranks, like stuff a mouse in someone's pocket or stick a dish to a table cloth with workman's glue, causing a huge disaster when someone tries to pick it up. All innocent pranks at most, but that was how everyone knew her and more often than not, when she was younger her father would ground her for punishment, but she always found a way out of it.

And then there was Rachel, shy quiet Rachel. More like the runt of the litter, she was one of few words and always just tagged along because Amity and Betty insisted. Rachel only had a father; her mother died giving birth to her. Her father eventually married Elsa, a widow with two sons, who she never got on with. They were two brats and she ended up spending more time with her friends than her own family and over the years, the trio had become the best of friends

Betty giggled and Amity squirmed on the bale of hay, "I bet you David looks like that when he takes his shirt off," she said pointing to the male model in the fashion magazine.

Amity giggled, "It's scandalous! If your dad knew you had these, he'll shun us all," she said in jest.

Rachel, curious as ever, was sitting on the left, also peeking at the magazine, one of the few they kept hidden in the barn under one of the wooden floor slats. They always snuck to the barn to page through the magazines and weigh every other man in their town up against the likes of models that posed so shamelessly with nothing but pair of underpants on.

"*Jah!* Well he doesn't know now does he?" Betty said and paged through a few more pages.

Rachel would never admit it out rightly but she also felt a slight tingle of excitement when she looked at these magazines, they were not overly crude, but they showed more flesh than she had ever seen in her life. Maybe it was because of this, that they were all still single, she thought. Comparing the local boys to those men were like comparing apples with onions.

A sudden noise quickly alerted them and Betty shoved the magazine behind the bale of hay they were seated on. Both Amity and Betty grabbed their egg baskets, while Rachel stood around looking as guilty as ever.

"Betty, are you girls here?"

It was Betty's father who called, and Rachel's stomach lurched, if the Bishop had any idea what they were up to they will be in so much trouble.

"We're here *daed*!" Betty called and dusted the hay off of her dress, "We were caught in the rain, and was waiting for it to pass," she said as her Bishop Gunther appeared.

"I thought so, well I have come to get you girls home, the storm is a long way from being over," he said and handed each of them a rain coat, "Better we hurry, or the storm will catch up with us," he urged them as he let each one of the girls walk towards the barn door ahead of him.

The sky was dark and it wasn't just a summer shower, it was a downpour that looked more like a waterfall from heaven. Heavy drops struck the ground tunnelling into the earth. Up ahead stood the buggy, which didn't offer much or any shelter and Rachel wasn't so sure if they would make it to their respective homes in one piece. Betty was the first to step into the rain, followed by Amity. Bishop Gunther looked at her and nodded, and then in a huddled group the four of them ran towards the buggy, careful not to slip and fall.

Thankful that there was still some daylight to guide the way, the three girls clung to each other as Betty's father steered the buggy towards the house. Hardly able to see a few feet ahead of them and on a treacherous road that has been washed away in most places, Bishop Gunther was still able to make them feel at ease. He didn't even look worried, but then again, that was probably how a man of God should be, like Paul walking on water.

The buggy wheels rattled as they rode over rocks and muddy trenches formed by the mass of water running diagonally across the small road. And a trip that normally took less than fifteen minutes to travel, now seemed like an eternity. They were slowly making their way ahead through the stormy downpour, unbeknownst to Bishop Gunther, the road up ahead had turned into complete sludge and the moment the buggy reached it, the wheels simply slid into a deep trench on the side of the road, pulling the buggy, with the horse off and on to the side of the road. The girls screamed in panic as the buggy slowly leaned over to its side, threatening to topple over. Rachel was the first to clobber out and then helped the other two on to the road. Betty got out safely, but as Amity stumbled out of the buggy, she stepped in a hole and twisted her ankle.

"Ow!!" she cried out as she fell to the ground grabbing for her ankle.

"Amity!" Betty cried and ducked down to help her friend, "Where does it hurt?"

Bishop Gunther also hunched down and looked at her ankle, "It's quite swollen, I think you may have sprained it, can you try and step on it?"

Betty and her father helped Amity to her feet, but the moment she put weight on her injury, she cried out in agony.

"We will have to get you home, just lean on me and Betty" the Bishop said. He studied the state of the buggy, "The buggy will have to stay here until morning."

"But papa, we can hardly see in front of us," Betty lamented as she supported her friend.

"The Lord will light our way," Rachel said confidently and gave Betty a gentle reassuring squeeze.

With Amity supported by Bishop Gunther and Betty, and Rachel next to them carrying the egg baskets, they started down the path taking carful steps in the dark.

Through the stormy gale and rain that kept showering, they heard a galloping sound that sounded more like thunder coming towards them and the next moment, a man on horseback arrived completely drenched.

Rachel couldn't make out his face, but right now he was the best thing that could have happened to them.

"Bishop, Maryanne sent me to see what was keeping you," he shouted over the raging storm, "What happened to the buggy?"

Rachel took over from the Bishop, while he explained to the stranger exactly what had happened, and suggested that they come to recover the buggy in the morning once the rain has passed.

"Betty, you will have to get on the horse with Amity, Rachel you will walk with Uri and I," the Bishop instructed and then the stranger named Uri, helped Amity, and then Betty on to the horse.

Together they slowly made their way back to society, the first stop was Amity's house, where the Bishop helped to get her inside, and seen to, then it was Rachel's turn and finally Uri, Bishop Gunther and Betty made their way to the Bishop's house.

~*~

After Rachel had changed into her night dress and towel dried her wet hair, she deposited herself in front of the fire place. The night had turned out a complete disaster. She was sure it was punishment for their bad behaviour. Lusting like that over fictitious men and so on. She wrapped her quilt around her shoulders and reached for her bible. She knew better than to let her judgement be influenced by anyone. Despite the guilt, she somehow found her mind drifting to the stranger who came to their aid. She still couldn't see his face clearly, but she was sure he was handsome, and strong.

She shook her head to chase away the thoughts and closed her eyes, and said a silent prayer of repentance. She was never going to look at those magazines again.

Chapter 2

The sun broke through the parted curtains in Rachel's room and she pinched her eyes shut. The night before had taken its toll on her, and resulted in her oversleeping when there was still so much to do. She was yet to feed the geese and get ready to go to the local market to deliver the eggs she had collected the day before, but she simply had no will power.

"Rachel!" Her step-mother called from the kitchen, "Come have your breakfast!"

Rachel covered her eyes with her forearm and sighed. She just needed a few more minutes of sleep, but she knew where her priorities lay. She willed herself out of bed and rushed around the room to get ready for the day. By the time she got to the kitchen her mother had already cleaned the dishes, and Rachel's breakfast was waiting.

"The Bishop and his friend were here earlier," Elsa commented in passing, "Looks like you girls had a rough night."

"Yeah, we got caught in the storm," she mumbled.

So the stranger is one of the Bishop's friends, which means he was old, she thought to herself.

"Apparently Amity had twisted her ankle quite badly, but she will be fine in a few days."

"I figured. She stepped in a hole when she tried to get out of the buggy, we couldn't see much."

Elsa came to sit at the table with her, "You girls need to be more careful, things could have been a lot worse."

Sometimes Rachel couldn't help but wonder what Elsa's agenda really was. At times she treated her like a stranger, barely paying attention to her, and other times she came across all motherly. And all this time Rachel had no choice but to keep her own emotions all bottled up.

"We will," Rachel said and stood up to wash her plate, "I'm taking the eggs to the market, is there anything you need me to do?"

"Oh not to worry about the eggs, I've already sold delivered them this morning."

Rachel felt as if she could crush the plate in her hands. Those eggs were her eggs, her income. She was saving money for herself, and now Elsa had taken the little bit she could earn for herself.

"Thank you," she said tight lipped without turning around.

"I hope you don't mind, your father does need some money to buy that new gas stove so, I figured every penny would help."

"Of course," Rachel turned around this time, with a fake smile plastered on her face, "I'll just get more eggs to get money for my new dress."

"Why on earth would you need a new dress?" Elsa said with mock surprise, "Don't you have enough as it is?"

Rachel was slowly starting to lose her temper, but she fought hard to remain calm, "I only have three dresses, and I need one for church, the others are all worn and faded."

Elsa laughed, "It's not like you'll be catching anyone's eye, and you're past the point of marriage. You're already considered a spinster."

"I'm only twenty-two, the same age my mother married," Rachel protested.

"And see how that turned out."

Elsa had barely said the words when her sons, Caleb and Alfred came into the kitchen, and Rachel had to hide her anger. She simply scooped up her empty egg baskets and stormed out of the house. How that woman dared say such heartless things and get away with it, was beyond her she thought as she marched determinedly in no particular direction. But as the anger subsided, it was replaced by doubt. Maybe it was too late for her to marry, but then the same applied to Betty and Amity, they were both the same age. Obviously living in Derby Creek wasn't much help either, there were far more women than men here, and unless they had gatherings from nearby towns, chances of finding a suitor was slim.

First of all there was Betty, who insisted that she was waiting for Mr Right, she refused to settle for less, then there's Amity who also had her own ideas of a suitor, and the few men that did ask for her hand in the past, were coldly turned down because she was just not interested. Rachel always thought that Amity was the kind who would go on a Rumspringa if her father allowed her, out of the three friends, she was the adventurous one.

Rachel grunted a loud oomph as she collided with someone sending her baskets flying. Thankfully they were empty; otherwise they would both have been covered in egg yolk. She stumbled back and started to apologize profusely when she swallowed her words, and a pair of very strong hands cupped her shoulders.

"Are you alight?" the young man asked, and offered her a lopsided smile.

"Jah, I am fine, I-I wasn't paying attention, I'm sorry," she said struggling to breathe.

"It's quite alright, you were miles away there for a second, I'm Uri, Rachel right?" he said and released her as he tucked his thumbs into his suspenders.

Uri, the name immediately rang a bell. He was Bishop Gunther's friend, but how? He was so young, she wondered.

"How do you know my name?" she asked foolishly.

"I came to your rescue last night in the storm, but I suppose you won't recognise me, it was rather dark."

"Oh! Oh right, yes. Well... um, I'll be going now. Thank you, I mean sorry, I... I have to go."

Rachel just about ran away from him, she had acted like a complete and utter fool, stuttering over her words like a second grader having to do an oral assignment. No wonder she was single. She couldn't sit in the company of a man without feeling awkward. As she hurried away she could feel his eyes burn into the back of her, but she refused to glance back. The farther she got away the quicker her out of control heart and raging butterflies would quieten down.

"Rachel!" It was Betty who waved her down, "Where are you heading?"

"Eggs!"

"You're going to Eggs?" Betty giggled.

"No, ugh, I'm going to collect eggs silly," she corrected herself as Betty fell into step next to her, "How is Amity doing?"

"She's fine, but you look like you've seen a ghost, why are you in such a hurry," Betty said as she tried to keep up to Rachel's pace.

"I need to sell enough eggs to buy a new dress. The cow sold all the eggs I collected yesterday."

"What a cow, did she not even ask you?"

"Does she ever?"

The rest of the way, the two friends walked in silence, Betty on her own planet, and Rachel trying to get Uri out of her mind. She hadn't expected him to be so young, nor did she expect him to know her name. The night before was a bit of a blur with everything going on, and she mostly remembered walking beside Bishop Gunther while Uri guided the horse by its reins with Amity and Betty on horseback.

"Is Uri your..."

"Don't you think Uri is..."

They both said at the same time and then burst out laughing.

"Uri is so handsome," Betty continued, "The last time I saw him was when we were kids. His family has been in Germany for the past few years."

"I didn't expect him to be so young," Rachel said, "Are they staying here?"

"Only Uri, he's staying at our house and is helping papa with a few things."

Rachel could hear by Betty's tone that she was keen on Uri, and she knew by the seam of her dress, that Amity will be just as taken by him.

One of them will most certainly catch his eyes, she thought and smiled softly. Her friends or at least one of them deserved a good strong man to care for them.

She dismissed the notion of Uri straight away, knowing that she would never stand a chance. She could hardly string together a proper sentence when she bumped into him earlier.

Chapter 3

Amity humped along with a crutch in one hand, while Betty excitedly skipped besides them. For the first time in who knows how long, Betty and Amity had made some effort to look presentable, both of them had brand new dresses. It was the Friday night frolic, where most boys got to voice their intentions.

Betty was nervous; as usual she was shy and nervous. She never liked these events much, she did not trust the thing called love, her father loved once, he had promised his her mother that he would make sure she was taken care of, but now years later, all she had to remember her mother by was a single letter, and a lifetime of regret. Elsa was kind in some ways, but she was jealous of Betty, and Betty never did much right in her eyes.

The people from the surrounding farms started to arrive, old and young, in the middle of the big barn the table was set as always. Food in excess was spread across the table, along with lanterns casting a dim glow over everything.

"Have you seen how handsome Uri is?" Betty whispered under her breath.

Amity giggled and shifted in her chair, "I know right? I can still feel his hands on my hips as he helped me on to the horse."

"Oh and weren't they the biggest stronger hands ever?" Betty swooned.

"I'm going to make a play for him you know?" Amity murmured under her breath.

"No you're not, I am, and I've already spent some quality time with him."

Betty wagged her brows and reached for bunch of grapes.

"You can't eat now, we have to say thanks first," Amity said slapping Betty's hand.

"Oh please, no one is even looking."

Betty listened to her friends as they cooed over the newcomer and she opted not to show any interest. They had reason to try and win his affection, she had none. She will see this night through and make the best of a bad situation. Besides, she had a lot more on her mind. Maybe it was time she accepted the fact that she was a spinster, and she figured it was time she spoke to the Bishop and go his take on her moving out of her paternal home into her own. She could always offer her help as a teacher. She knew how to read, in fact she loved reading. She could go spend time at the local school and read to the youngsters, even help the school teachers to give extra lessons in literacy.

"Rachel!" Amity's voice broke into her thoughts.

"Oh... sorry I wasn't listening," she apologised.

"I was saying, maybe all three of us should play for Uri, we can see which one he picks."

Rachel raised her brows, "He's not up for auction, it's a silly game you're wanting to play."

"Stop being such a drab! It will be fun."

No it won't, she thought. The first thing that is bound to happen is that Uri will pick either Betty or Amity, then that will leave one or the other angry and disappointed, ruining a friendship of many years.

"I'm not a drab, I'm just saying. What if he picks Betty, then you'll be angry, not?"

Amity rolled her eyes, "You take things way to seriously, if he picks Betty, then so be it, I'm hardly desperate to marry."

"Come on Rachel, it will be fun; besides, maybe he shows no interest in any of us, then at least we know we all tried."

Betty worried her lip and looked down at her hands, "I don't know, I suppose no harm can come of it." She for one knew that she won't be the least bit phased if he picked Amity or Betty, because she knew she stood no chance.

Amity shoved her elbow into Rachel's ribs and gestured with her head towards the door. Talk of the devil, Uri was heading straight down the path on the opposite side of the table with his eyes fixed on them. And once again the sight of him made her heart race and as she watched him approach it was as if all else around her faded. She had tunnel vision and it was only him looking straight at her. When he finally stopped and took a seat directly opposite her she averted her eyes immediately. Of course, Amity kicked her under the table and Rachel cleared her throat uncomfortably.

"*Hallo* Uri," she said.

"*Hoe gaan het*, Rachel?" he smiled.

She only nodded, her tongue felt like led in her mouth, and her palms were sweaty.

Betty and Amity both fell right into conversation, putting their best foot forward while Rachel wanted nothing but to flee. Soon enough the evening got on the way, with youngsters all frolicking and enjoying the event. Uri made sure he mingled with everyone and never let on that he was interested in any of them in particular, which was funny, since Betty put her best foot forward and out rightly told him he had beautiful eyes.

As the evening drew to a close and most of the people had left, the last remaining few spent the rest of the time talking about the up and coming barn raising event. Uri was still seated across from Rachel, and Betty and Amity had moved closer to where Bishop Gunther was. He was playing the harmonica, which was probably the only instrument allowed in the community, but still sounded like heaven.

"So Rachel, have you always lived here?" Uri asked curiously as he picked on some of the bread sticks on his plate.

"*Jah*, I was born here," she said and offered him a shy smile.

"I'm surprised I don't remember you?"

"I'm not exactly the most memorable of all," she laughed.

"Oh but you are, you are a very beautiful woman."

Rachel blushed profusely and covered the side of her face with her hand, "Thank you," she mumbled.

"Can I pick you up for church on Sunday?"

Shocked at his request, Rachel shifted uncomfortably in her seat and worried her lip, as tempting as it was, she wasn't so sure if it was a good idea. But then again, Betty and Amity did say that they should all try and win his affection. She looked down at her empty plate and smiled. Perhaps it was time she stepped out of her comfort zone and tried dating at least, after all, he was simply going to take her to church, and it wasn't like he was proposing to her at all.

"Sure," she said and then got up, "I have to go now. I will see you around."

She saw his mouth open and close, but she rushed away regardless. She said her goodbyes to her friends and the rest of the community who were all still in the barn and headed home. Her mind was racing and her heart even more. For the life of her she couldn't understand what Uri saw in her. *You're a beautiful woman* – he had said, and it made her feel as if she was about to fly into the night sky on wings of angels. No boy, or man for that matter, had ever paid her such a compliment, and coming from someone as handsome and Uri, made her tummy do strange things.

Chapter 4

Uri was up and ready long before dawn on Sunday, making sure his buggy was clean and that he too was dressed in his best church clothes. He couldn't deny the fact that he felt bad for Betty, she had shown her affection so openly, but there was just no chemistry between them. Unlike Rachel, Betty was just too flamboyant to his liking. She was a pretty woman, but not even nearly as pretty as Rachel. Rachel was unusually pretty, with red hair that always seemed so perfectly plated and rolled up under her prayer cap, with loose strands that tickled her cheeks. The slight dusting of freckles across her nose, that spread to her cheeks made her even prettier, almost innocent not to mention the way she blushed every time he spoke to her.

He was quite surprised when she accepted his request to start off with, but pleased nonetheless.

The first night he saw the shy girl, with her baskets filled with eggs, he was intrigued. She was in control despite the stormy weather and their predicament, and even when he lifted the other two on to the horse, she never uttered as single complaint. She walked quietly next to them as if she was taking a stroll. Not even the rain slanting heavily against them broke through her composure. Maybe it was the way she kept to herself, or the way her eyes lit up the next day when he bumped into her, he wasn't quite sure himself, but if he had to pin it to one thing, it was God's will. It was God's will that he returned to Derby Creek after all these years and God had sent the storm so that he could meet his future wife.

"Uri, you're up early," Betty said as she entered the kitchen where he was having his morning tea.

"Jah, up and ready for church," he said and grinned excitedly.

She came to sit next to him and perched her chin on her hand, looking at him all dreamy eyed. Shifting slightly to get some distance, he smiled and shoved the plate of rusks closer to her.

"I'm on my way to collect Rachel for church," he announced, not sure how Betty would react.

From day one, she had made it no secret that she fancied him; neither did Amity, so it was better if he got it out in the open before either of them got their hopes up.

"Rachel?" Betty said scrunching up her face, "Have you asked her then?"

He nodded and took the last sip of his tea, "Jah, she's a shy one, but she accepted my offer."

Betty scratched her head and slumped back in her chair, and Uri could just imagine what thoughts were flitting through her mind, hoping that this would not ruin their friendship. But when Betty stood up and held her hand up for a high-five, he grinned.

"She's a dear friend, but a nervous wreck, you best make sure you treat her right," Betty grinned, "She's had a lot of hardship with that stepmother of hers."

Uri frowned, tempted to ask about this stepmother, but held back. If anyone was going to tell him about Rachel, it was Rachel herself. He would want for no secrets or tall tales to come from anyone other than her.

He looked at the clock against the wall in the kitchen and took his hat, nodded at Betty and headed out. For a man nearing his thirties, he felt like teenager himself.

~*~

Rachel waited outside for Uri's arrival and her stomach was doing wild flips, while her heart was missing beats every so often trying to keep up the pace. She had never entertained the advances of a man, and had no idea how to behave in the presence of one who had made his intensions clear. A boy simply did not offer a girl a ride in his buggy unless he was interested in her as more than a friend. This was serious business. She also omitted to let her father know, because she knew that Elsa would have a hundred and one things to say about it. She shifted on the swing chair changing her position, trying to find the one that made her feel most at ease, but her body felt awkward. Her arms felt as if they were too long, her legs felt numb and overall her body and mind appeared to be disconnected. Tired of trying to figure out the best seating position she stood up and paced up and down the porch, and then finally she opted for leaning against the pillar. Just in time too, as she heard the nearing rumble of a buggy, which could only have been Uri.

When he came to a stop in front of her gate, she quickly rushed down the stairs.

"Morning Rachel, you look lovely today," Uri said as he climbed out and came around to help her in.

"Good morning," she said softly.

"Did you sleep well?"

"Jah, I did, thank you."

It took her some time to loosen up and say more than four words at a time, but Uri had this amazing ability to make her feel free. With him she didn't have to count every word, or watch her tongue. She could just say what she wanted. On their way to church, he asked her about the things she likes most. The talked about her life, and her family, she didn't feel like she needed to hide anything from him at all. She even admitted how she felt about Elsa, which made her feel less restricted. At church, they didn't sit next to each other, but Betty and Amity were curious as ever.

"So he picked you did he?" Amity whispered under her breath.

"I don't know, maybe," Rachel murmured.

"You're blind as a bat; everyone can see he likes you."

Rachel blushed and kept her head down, her friends were impossible and as much as she tried to pay attention to the service she couldn't. If it wasn't for Betty or Amity, whispering to her under their breaths, it was the sure awareness of Uri watching her. And that did not go unnoticed by her friends either.

By the time the service had come to an end, Rachel couldn't wait to get outside to catch a breath of fresh air, and steal a moment for herself, but it was short lived.

"You never told us you're meeting a boy?" Elsa said as she came to stand next to Rachel.

"I didn't know I needed your permission," Rachel said blankly.

"Well I suppose you are old enough to make your own, but you know, Albert will be very disappointed that you never told him."

Rachel knew exactly what Elsa was playing at, and this time she was not going to let the woman who pretends to care throw any hurdles in her way.

"I think he'll live, and you should be too pleased that I won't be a bother to you for much longer."

Talk about rushing into things, Rachel thought as she hurried away from Elsa, it wasn't as if Uri was going to ask for her hand in marriage, they hardly knew each other. But even if that wasn't the case, whatever happened, come the beginning of winter, she would move out anyway and start her own life, with or without a husband.

Chapter 5

Uri had spent most of the time getting to know Rachel, and the more he got to know her, the more he was convinced that she was the perfect wife for him. He had spent almost every evening visiting with Rachel and in the past few months since they started their courtship he got to know a woman, who despite her adversities in life, rose above it all. Her stepmother no longer tried to boss her around, and her father was too pleased that his only daughter is finally blooming.

It was a perfect autumn day; the ground was covered in a carpet of reds and golds that reminded him of Rachel. He had already asked her father for her hand in marriage, and although it didn't quite follow the custom of dating for an extended period, he saw no reason to wait. They were both adults who were in love and certain of one thing, their own happiness.

As usual he waited patiently for Rachel to exit the house, and like two curious toddlers Amity and Betty was not far away either. They had both come to terms with the fact that he had made his choice, and they were extra supportive of Rachel too. As he whispered a silent prayer for guidance, Rachel made her appearance as if the Lord had answered his prayer. Today was the day he was going to ask her for her hand in person.

"Good morning Uri," she said and her smile lit up his world.

"Morning to you Rachel, you look absolutely radiant today," he complemented her and it earned him an even wider smile.

"I made myself a new dress, do you like it?"

"It's beautiful," he said and held out his hand.

He could already imagine the gasps and giggles coming from the two friends as he struggled to find the right words. He had rehearsed it so well, but now here in the moment, he was at a loss for words.

"Are you alright?" she asked and placed the back of her hand against his cheek, "You look flustered."

Uri cleared his throat and caught her hand, keeping it against his cheek, "I'm fine, but there is something I would like to ask you."

Rachel tilted her head and her hazel eyes sparkled with curiosity as she waited for him to speak.

"Go on!" Betty shouted from across the road!

Uri closed his eyes and smiled, they weren't helping him at all.

"Uri?" Rachel said softly, "What is it?"

He took a deep breath, and then took both her hands in his, "Rachel, I have spoken to your father, and I would be honoured if you would agree to become my wife."

The way Rachel's expression changed from being concerned to completely surprise was priceless. She didn't have to answer him at all, because the way her lips tugged into a wide smile and her eyes filled with tears, he knew she wouldn't turn him down.

Rachel flung her arms around his neck and buried her face in the crook of his neck and whispered, "I thought you'd never ask."

Uri chuckled, "I was hoping you would accept."

"Why would I not?" she said and smiled lovingly up at him.

THE AMISH HEART

ABBY BARKER

"I'll only be gone for a little while, Ma. It's a seasonal position so it's only for the summer. I'll be home before you know it."

"Soon isn't soon enough, Annie. I want you here with Pa and I working around the house, not in some zoo."

"Nancy pulled all sorts of strings to get me this job. You told me I could go on rumspringa. Why are you trying to take it back?"

Annie's mother looked at her with defeated eyes but didn't say a word. She knew how much planning and excitement her daughter put into this getaway. There would be no way to convince her hardheaded girl to revise her plan now. She let out a deep sigh and handed back the tote bag she had been clinging to as an attempt to force Annie to stay.

"Thanks, Ma. This will be good for me, and you. Nancy's going to be here any minute now and I really do need to finish packing."

Annie kissed her mother on the cheek and went back to meticulously choosing which of her old-fashioned Amish outfits could pass as casual English fashion. It wasn't easy. Other than a handful of pajama sets that she convinced her mother to let her buy – only for wearing around the house – she mostly had long skirts and shawls. She'd have to go shopping with Nancy when they got to the city.

Annie felt a wave of excitement and nerves wash over her. Not only was she starting a job working with animals, her one true passion, but she'd be doing it in Chicago. She thought back on the times when she and Nancy were kids and they talked about getting an apartment together somewhere exciting. It wasn't until she met Nancy that she learned anything about English life at all.

Nancy's family is English, but living so close to their town her parents were longtime family friends of Annie's neighbors. The Millers didn't have any children of their own, so when Nancy came to visit they'd send her over to Annie's to play. Even coming from two different worlds, the two girls had plenty in common. They liked climbing trees, playing hide and seek in the field, and most of all playing veterinarian. They would wander around the farm diagnosing the animals with any number of made-up illnesses and curing them with equally fictional remedies. The goats were easily susceptible to Pink-horn-itis, which was easily cured by a health dose of fairy dust, while the horses could often be found suffering from the Tap Dancing Flu. That illness had to run its course, but singing an upbeat song and dancing along could expedite the healing process.

The only difference between them was when they were old enough to go to college Nancy was the only one who went. Annie's parents instead she stay at home and learn how to take care of the farm. While Nancy worked towards her veterinary degree, Annie cooked, cleaned, and tended to the livestock. Annie understood why her parents didn't let her go to school, but that didn't mean she was happy about it. So when Nancy heard of an open assistant zookeeper position at the city zoo where she was interning she jumped at the chance for Annie to apply. The job only lasted a couple months, filling in when needed during the zoo's busy summer season, which made it a perfect fit for Annie. She'd have to go back to her town eventually or risk getting shunned by her entire community, including her parents.

Nancy eventually convinced her bosses that Annie would be a good fit for the job, what with her experience working with farm animals and above all else, her passion. They agreed she would come stay with Nancy in the city while she worked. Their childhood dreams were finally coming true, even if it was temporary. Annie's daydreaming was interrupted by a honk from outside. She shoved whatever item of clothing she had in her hand into her bag and bolted out the door. Nancy jumped out of the driver's seat and ran to meet her friend. The two girls jumped up and down squealing, both equally excited to finally live together.

"Annie, Annie, Annie, Ann! Get your ass in the car!"

Nancy clasped her hand over her mouth and looked around nervously hoping Annie's parents weren't within earshot. Luckily, they weren't as quick to great her as Annie was.

"Whoops. I'll try and keep the swearing to a minimum until we're on the road."

"Well let's get on the damn road already!"

The girls fell into a fit of laughter just as Annie's parents joined them on the lawn.

"What could you two possibly be laughing about already?"

"Nothing, Ma. We're just excited is all," Annie said, stifling a giggle. Her mother had calmed down considerably since their conversation earlier, but jokes involving swear words would only upset her again. She uncrossed her arms to give her daughter a hug.

"Be good and be careful, sweetheart. Zoo animals are not like farm animals, and English people are not like Amish people. No offence, Nancy, I just want you to be prepared for city life."

"Ma, I think you're being a little dramatic. It's not like the English are a completely different species."

Annie mother just pursed her lips and stayed silent. She didn't want to argue with her daughter right before she left for the summer.

"I'll be fine. Nancy will be there."

"That's what I'm afraid off," she teased playfully.

After a final round of hugs for her parents, and a gentle scolding from Annie's mother to Nancy about not corrupting her little girl, the pair set out for Chicago. They only made it about two blocks before erupting into laughter again. It had been a few months since they'd seen each other last and they were overflowing with pent up energy. Annie had her friends in town, but they were often more reserved and frankly more boring than Nancy. She enjoyed Amish life just as much as the next girl, but sometimes she needed an outlet.

"Annie-bananie, you are going to crap your pants when you see the city. The only horses and buggies you're going to see will be shuttling tourists between steakhouses and the Sears Tower."

"I don't really have a lot of clothes so I'm going to have to be careful about how much crapping I'm doing in them."

"I'll take you downtown and get you plenty of new outfits to crap in. Don't you worry."

The city was a few hours drive from Annie's town but it felt like no time at all. The two girls chatted away nonstop for the entire trip. Nancy went through her entire mental list of favorite restaurants, shops, and museums in between Annie's lamenting about how stifling her parents have been ever since she decided to spend the summer in Chicago. While they respected her decision, they didn't like it. They spent the last few weeks doing everything they could to convince her to stay and giving her the cold shoulder when she wouldn't change her mind. She felt guilty at times, but knew this was the right choice for her.

When the skyline finally came into view Annie gasped. The staggered peaks of the downtown buildings formed a giant fence standing between where she was now and where she wanted to be. The sight overwhelmed her. She'd never seen anything so incredibly massive in her entire life. The biggest building in her town was a two-story barn. She hoped the giant fence she pictured also had a gate.

Nancy drove into the city, the streets slowly narrowing, until she came to a modest apartment building next to a wide, green park. Just on the other side of the park was a seemingly never-ending lake.

"We're home!" Nancy yelled, pulling into a parking space next to the building. "Wait until you see the view from our living room. You can almost see Michigan across the lake!"

Annie was still reeling from all the new things she saw in this state, she didn't know if she'd be able to handle another whole state.

***

After excitedly riding an elevator for the first time, flipping through every channel on TV, and marveling at Nancy's expansive and colorful wardrobe Annie worked up an appetite. There wasn't always a huge variety when it came to meals back home. The food was always good

– fresh vegetables, milk from their cow, bread straight from the oven – but supper could get a bit repetitive over time. She knew Chicago to be filled with every type of cuisine imaginable, but there was one thing she'd been dying to try ever since she decided to move in with Nancy.

"Nance, we have to get deep dish pizza, like, right now. If I don't have a slice of famous Chicago deep dish in front of me soon I'll totally lose it."

"Okay, okay chill out. We'll get you that cheesy, delicious slice. We gotta go to Lou Malnati's. It's the absolute best."

"Yes, that's all I want. Maybe I should change first before we go."

Annie realized that she was still wearing her long, black skirt and button-up blouse from back home. The conservative outfit didn't seem to her to be the most fashionable option but she didn't have much else to choose from. Luckily, Nancy was there to reassure her.

"No way. You look rad and a little bit vintage-y in that getup. People are gonna think you're some kind of fashion icon."

She linked her arm through Annie's and pulled her towards the door. A true Chicagoan, Nancy had no time to waste when it came to deep dish. The girls walked through the bustling city talking and laughing, the excitement from the day's events not quite worn off. Annie was fascinated by how much life there was in streets. Shops and restaurants had their doors open, families walked together through the park, and friends just like them made their ways to get their own delicious dinners. The contrast to her little town was striking. She only saw groups of people this large when she went to the market or church, but just walking through the streets she encountered the odd farmer or woman also on their way into town, but nothing so lively as this and never at night. She couldn't help but smile at the various people she passed, and to her surprise, they more often than not smiled back. She couldn't wait to tell her mother how wrong she was about people in the city not being friendly.

At the restaurant they were seated right away, despite it being fairly crowded. Annie didn't even have to look at the menu. She excitedly told the waiter exactly what she wanted the moment they sat down. While they waited for their food she noticed a young man across the restaurant looking over at her. He had dark, curly hair and eyes to match. Every time she caught him glancing over he'd smile a little before returning to his meal. Eventually Annie couldn't take it anymore. She had to know why he was doing this.

"Nancy, do you see that guy over there? He keeps staring at me and smiling. It's super weird."

"He probably thinks you're cute! You should go over and talk to him."

"No way! That would be even weirder."

"No it wouldn't. He keeps looking at you. He obviously wants to talk to you. At the very least you can ask him what his deal is."

Annie glanced over toward the man and noticed he was staring at her once again. That was the last straw. She stood up from the table and marched over to him.

"Excuse me, I couldn't help but notice that you couldn't help but notice me. Can I ask why you keep staring at me?"

"I'm sorry! I didn't mean to freak you out. I just saw your clothing and thought you might be Amish. I'm Amish too, or at least I was, or maybe I might be again. I still haven't decided yet, but it's nice to see a familiar face or skirt, I mean."

Annie's face flushed. She didn't expect him to be so friendly and felt a little embarrassed for approaching him so hostilely.

"I should have just come up to talk to you instead of making you storm over like that. It's not the best first impression, I know. My name's Sean. What are you doing so far from home?"

"I'm staying with a friend of mine," she gestured behind her toward Nancy. "I start working at the zoo tomorrow."

"The zoo! That's definitely not what I was expecting but I'd love to hear more. Would you want to meet up for coffee sometime, when you're not busy tending to the animals of course?"

Annie walked over to this man expecting to tell him off, but instead he's asked her on a date? Chicago was exceeding her expectations. She felt a little guilty dating outside of her community, but Sean said he was Amish, or used to be at least. That was close enough, right? She decided what her parents didn't know wouldn't hurt them.

"I'm sure I'll have some free time while they sleep. Coffee sounds lovely."

"Great! Give me your phone number and I'll call you sometime."

"That might be a problem. I don't actually have a phone yet, but I can give you my friend's number and you can reach me there."

"Ah, you're fresh from Amish land then," Sean teased. "Her number will work just fine."

Annie recited the digits off to him before saying a polite goodbye and returning to her table. When she got there Nancy practically crawled over the table to get the details of their interaction.

"Who is that guy? You were over there for a long time. Why was he staring at you? Was I right? Does he think you're cute? Do you think he's cute?"

Annie relayed the conversation in acute detail, still excited about the prospect of her first big city date. Nancy nodded along happily, interjecting occasionally.

"No way! What are the frickin' chances that on your first night here you'd run into another Amish person, or formally Amish or whatever. I mean, of course he asked you on a date, too, you're frickin' amazing. Am I saying frickin' a lot again? I'm just so frickin' excited for you!"

Annie laughed. Nancy was almost more enthusiastic about this than she was.

"He's cute, right? Most of the guys I'm used to seeing are dressed for church."

"Oh yeah, he's definitely cute, like, super cute. You done good, my friend."

When Annie crawled into bed that night she had to force herself to sleep. She couldn't help but repeat the conversation with Sean over and over again in her head. It wasn't much, but it consumed her thoughts. As she drifted off she couldn't tell if the butterflies in her stomach were mostly because she'd start her new job in the morning, or if they were from him.

She was awoken the next morning by Nancy tickling her feet at the end of the bed.

"Get up Annie! The animals wait for no man, or woman."

Annie groaned and giggled before rolling out of bed and slowly getting dressed. Nancy had made coffee and was waiting for her in the kitchen.

"Either chug a cup of hot coffee our grab a to-go mug out of the cabinet and take it with you. Don't want to be late on your first day, or my one hundredth."

"Is it really your one hundredth day of work?"

"Man, you really do need some coffee. I'm only joking with you, but seriously let's go. It's only a twenty minute walk from here."

Annie filled a thermos with coffee and the two girls flew out the door. She was glad to have the brisk walk to wrangle in her nerves. This was going to be her first official job that also happened to be her dream. With the tons of excitement she felt also came a lot of pressure. Most of all, if she screwed up then she'd have to face her mother's "I told you so." It turned out she had nothing to worry about however because when they finally made it through the entrance of the zoo they were greeted by the most warm and welcoming zookeeper. Kyra was a pleasantly plump blonde woman with as much passion for animals as for hospitality. She began her introduction as Nancy politely excused herself – with a wink and reassuring shoulder pat to Annie – from the conversation as she was needed elsewhere.

"Annie! We're so happy to have you here. Nancy talked endlessly about you and your love for animals, we absolutely couldn't pass up the chance to invite you. My name's Kyra and I'm going to show you around today. I run HR here at the zoo so as long as you're doing your job and doing it well you unfortunately won't have to see me much after today! Let's get you your uniform and then I'll introduce you to some of our residents and your supervisor. You two will have plenty to talk about. He's Amish too! You'll be working mostly with the big cats, but I'll show you everything!"

Kyra slipped that fact seamlessly into her on boarding speech but Annie caught it immediately. Her new boss was Amish, or used to be. Is this Nancy got her the job? Also, what were the chances that she'd meet two Amish men within days of getting to the city? Was she some sort of magnet for people like her?

After changing into her new uniform, Annie followed Kyra around the zoo as she breathlessly explained the inner workings of the place as well as each of the animals' personalities in detail.

"Daphne and Dylan are our river otters and they spend most of their day playing tag in the pool and hamming it up for the guests. Those two a real attention seekers, let me tell you. They'll swim back and forth against the glass just trying to get someone to look at them."

Eventually they made it to the bear enclosure. Two brown bears slept cozily under a tree together, shaded by the branches above. They made soft noises in their sleep but were otherwise completely still.

"Now these two don't look like much right now but when they're awake boy are they trouble. They're not bad bears by any means, just mischievous. Don't turn your back on them for one second, even through the fence. They want whatever you have and will snack food right out of your hands. They're not trying to hurt you but they're bears. They can't help it. Oh, and their names are Ben and Jerry. We rescued them from a man who really liked ice cream and owning animals that shouldn't be kept as pets."

Annie watched their furry backs move up and down as the breathed. Even from outside the enclosure the bears were impressive. She couldn't wait to see them in action. She wondered when that might be.

"When do I start with my actual duties?"

"Well, we have a few more animals and a handful of people left to introduce you to today, but I'll drop you off with Andrew in a bit. He's a little shy, but a good boss. I think he prefers to spend his time with the cats rather than other people, but he's a real sweetheart. He'll show you the ropes!"

Annie followed Kyra around the zoo for a little while longer, meeting different keepers and animals along the way, before making it to the big cathouse. Once inside, Kyra lead them to a basement room set up like a restaurant kitchen. A surprisingly tall, blonde man stood at a silver counter hacking away at a hunk of meat. He didn't appear to notice them walk in, or he at least didn't acknowledge them.

"Andrew, this is your new assistant zookeeper, Annie. I want you to show her all it is you do around here."

Now that he had been directly addressed, Andrew looked away from his task and flashed the two women a bright smile.

"Nice to meet you, Annie. Want to chop up some raw meat with me?"

Kyra smiled and said, "That's the spirit!" before leaving Annie and Andrew alone in the prep kitchen. Andrew wordlessly gestured at the sink, seeming to indicate Annie should wash her hands before joining in. She rushed over to it, eager to make a good impression but nervous about being alone in a room with a man. The only men she was permitted to be alone with back home were family members, and even then only the close ones like her father and grandfather. She knew it wasn't a big deal in an English work place, but she couldn't help but feel a faint blush wash over her cheeks when she joined Andrew at the counter. It didn't help that she found his sandy hair and quiet eyes very attractive.

"So what you want to do is grab a hunk of meat, like this, and cut it into pieces, like this. Please don't be intimidated by skill level. I've been doing this for quite some time now."

He was clearly teasing her, and even though she understood this she still took extra care when cutting up her first piece. His gentle humor relaxed her nerves a bit and she felt comfortable enough to tease him right back.

"Is this right? Should I hold the knife by the blade?"

"Oh, yes. Everyone knows the handle is the best part of the knife for cutting meat. Just make sure to grip the blade extremely tight so that you don't lose control of it."

"Okay, perfect, I think I've got it. You're an excellent teacher."

"That's why they keep me around!"

They both laughed at that but then fell silent for a few moments as they continued their task. They were both comfortable with the silence but curious about each other. It didn't take long for Andrew to speak up.

"So, I hope you don't mind me asking this, but Nancy says you're Amish, right? What brings you to a zoo in Chicago?"

"I was about to ask you the same thing!" When Andrew looked surprised she clarified. "Kyra told me that 'we have a lot in common.'" They both laughed. "Nancy and I have been friends forever, but when she got the chance to go to school and get a veterinary degree I had to stay home and basically get a degree in housekeeping. When Nancy said she could get me this job I jumped at the chance to get out of there for a while before I have to marry a nice Amish boy and settle down."

"Another probing question, why do you want to go back? It doesn't sound like you want that kind of life, I know I didn't."

Annie thought about this for a moment. In a way, Andrew was right. An old-fashioned Amish marriage didn't really appeal to her, but she also couldn't imagine her life as anything other than Amish. There had to be a middle ground somewhere but she had no idea where that might be. Where did he find his middle ground? She could only reply, "I don't know. I guess we'll have to wait and see. Why did you decide to give it all up?"

"I raised cows on my family's farm. Just cows. Do you know how boring cows are? I wanted to do more than breed cattle and I couldn't believe that God would hate me for following my dreams, you know? My parents weren't happy, but I was."

They had finished the meat chopping and had now moved to putting it all into buckets to bring out to the big cats. Annie mentioned liking lions and Andrew agreed, but told her that the jaguar was his favorite.

"She's the queen of the big cat house. She's not as physically active as some of the other cats but when you look into her eyes as she's sitting up on her perch you can tell that she's looking back. She really sees you."

Annie felt an inadvertent smile spread across her face as she listened to the warmth and awe in Andrew's voice as he talked about the big cat. He truly cared for and admired the animals that he worked with. She found herself wondering if those feelings extended to any other parts of his life. Annie blushed when she realized where her mind had wandered. She wasn't even sure if Andrew was interested in her in that way, but part of her hoped he was. Finding romance wasn't her intention when she decided to come to Chicago but first with Sean and now Andrew she didn't know what to think.

Her mind raced as she and Andrew carried the heavy bucket of meat together to feed the big cats. Going from no romance in her life whatsoever to two potential crushes in 24 hours was overwhelming. She didn't know if she could handle one, let alone both men on her mind. She had almost convinced herself to give up on the idea of Andrew and focus on the guy who already showed an interest in her when Andrew's hand slipped on the bucket handle and brushed up against hers. Sparks like electric shocks shot up through her arm. That simple touch almost made her drop the bucket on the floor. She couldn't look at him directly but out of the corner of her eye she could see a small smile on his lips and a flush on his cheeks. He wasn't moving his hand. So much for forgetting about Andrew.

The walk to the enclosures felt like it lasted for miles when it was just down the hall. When the pair finally made it to the jaguar's cage and set down the bucket Annie felt like she could finally breath again. She didn't know what it was about him that made her feel so lightheaded but she was doing her best to control it. Andrew unlocked the door to the first part of the cage were they'd be able to toss the meat into the enclosure through the bars. It wasn't the most traditionally romantic spot, but the space was small and they had to stand shoulder to shoulder in order for them both to fit. The jaguar knew it was feeding time and began pacing back and forth along the bars. Seeing the predator up close sent a shiver down Annie's spine. The cat had all the majesty and intelligence Andrew described.

"Annie, meet Camilla. I like to think she gets excited to see me but I know it's really just the food. Want to toss her some meat?"

Annie nodded and stuck her hand in the bucket. The meat was cold and slimy but it didn't bother her. She grabbed a hunk and lobbed it through the bars and into the center of the enclosure. Camilla lunged for it and gobbled it up in one bite.

"She's fast!"

"If these bars weren't here she wouldn't hesitate to come after either of us and our bucket. We wouldn't get so far as the end of the hallway we came down before she pounced on us."

Annie looked startled.

"I'm only teasing! There's no way she's getting out of her enclosure."

When she didn't look convinced Andrew placed both hands on her shoulders for reassurance. Another shot of electricity ran through her entire body. He stared right into her eyes and she was frozen like a deer in headlights. He inched closer to her without removing his hands or breaking eye contact. She didn't move away. Before she could realize what was happening, Andrew pushed her up against the bars of Camilla's cage and kissed her passionately on the mouth. She felt Camilla brush past the backs of her legs from the other side of the bars. It was dangerous to be this close – to both the animal and this boy – but she kissed him back anyways. When he finally pulled away he looked sheepish.

"Whoops. I don't know what came over me. Some sort of animal instinct, I guess," they both laughed breathlessly. "Not exactly what you were expecting on your first day of work, huh?"

She touched her lips softly and chuckled. It was her first kiss.

"No. Not exactly."

Annie was shell-shocked. On the one hand, she never imagined a kiss would feel that way. Her parents and other adults in her community barely ever showed or talked about physical affection, which led her to believe it must not be that great. She was wrong. But on the other hand, she now had to think about Sean. She wasn't the type to see two men at once and now she had to make a choice.

Andrew, now embarrassed by his actions, took Annie's clipped response to mean wasn't interested. She thought it would be best to let him think this while she figured out what she wanted to do. It wouldn't be fair to lead him on if she really ended up liking Sean. Plus, she couldn't forget the expiration date on her time in Chicago. She'd have to go home in three months. Probably.

After feeding time, Kyra came back to collect Annie. There were a few more logistics and some paperwork they had to do before the end of the day. Andrew said an awkward "It was nice to meet you," to which Annie responded with a small smile and a wave. She hoped he didn't feel too embarrassed about the kiss. She wished she could tell him how much she enjoyed it without jumping the gun. She'd been in the city for less than 48 hours and things had already gotten complicated. For the first time since she arrived she felt a pang of longing for the simplicity of home.

A week went by before she heard from Sean. Andrew started to relax around her again. They'd joke around while preparing meals for all the big cats, tossing little chunks of raw meat at each other from across the room. It was flirtatious, but friendly – a speed Annie was comfortable with when it came to romance. She had all but given up on Sean and had even made plans with Andrew to hang out after work the next day when the boy from the pizza place called.

"ANNIE! Annie, Annie, Annie. You have a phone call. A good one!"

Nancy came barreling into Annie's room, cell phone raised above her head like an Olympic torch.

"Who is it?" Annie whispered, afraid the person on the other line could hear her friend's yelling.

"Oh, don't worry. I muted it. I think," she looked at the screen to double check. "Yep. Muted. It's that guy from Lou Malnati's! Sean, I think. He wants to talk to you! He wants to do *more* than talk to you."

Nancy winked, tossed the phone into Annie's hands, and waited in the doorway.

"Get out, loser! I'll tell you all about it afterwards. Don't sit there staring at me!"

After Nancy closed the door Annie took a deep breathe and unmated the phone.

"Hello?"

"Hey! Is this Annie?"

"Yes, it's me."

"Oh good. For a second I forgot you gave me your friend's number and thought it was a fake. I'm glad I was wrong. How are you?"

"I'm good. Just relaxing after a long day of chopping up animals to feed to other animals. I told you I work at a zoo, right? I'm not just a crazy person talking about chopping up animals."

She heard a laugh on the other line.

"You told me. Don't worry. Want to take a break from all that chopping and get dinner with me tomorrow?"

"Sure! As long as it's not raw meat."

Sean laughed again.

"Noted. I'll pick a place and text Nancy the details. See you tomorrow!"

It wasn't until after she hung up that she realized she'd already made plans with Andrew the next day. She had been so excited about Sean's call that she completely forgot. She should call Sean back and tell him her mistake, but did she want to?

"Nancy!"

Nancy appeared at Annie's bedroom door in less than a second. She'd been waiting outside.

"How did it go? Are you married now? Are you going to move away to a secluded island together?"

"What? No. Nancy, I have a little problem."

"What?"

"I might have accidentally agreed to hang out with Sean and Andrew at the same time."

"Oh boy, looks like you're gonna have to choose one. Who's it gonna be?"

"I don't know, Nancy! Sean was so nice at the restaurant, and so not my boss. But I can't forget that kiss. I mean, who knows if Andrew's even interested in me anymore though. Flinging hunks of raw meat at my head isn't exactly romantic."

"Well, duh, of course it is. Guys don't know how to deal with their feelings so they throw stuff at you and hope you figure it out."

"Ugh. What should I do?"

"Who do you like best?"

"I don't even know if I can like anyone at all! I have to go back home and marry a nice Amish boy like my mother wants anyways, not a formerly nice Amish boy. Why should I even bother?"

"Because it's fun! Plus, do you *have* to go back. I mean, I know it's been your plan and all but is that what you really want?"

"I don't know."

Annie slumped back onto her bed and closed her eyes. It's true, she couldn't imagine a life other than an Amish one but that didn't mean it wasn't possible. There would be plenty of consequences she'd have to face, but plenty of benefits too. She knew, though, that this was too big a choice to make based on a silly crush. She wouldn't give up being Amish for a boy, it would be for her.

Annie decided the next morning that she was going to try and hang out with both of them. She'd grab a coffee or something with Andrew after work and get out of there in time to meet Sean for dinner. She'd have to make a decision after that; Sean, Andrew, or neither.

After their shifts, Andrew took Annie to his favorite coffee shop nearby. The staff greeted him by name. He stopped in every morning before work to grab a cup. They ordered and found a table by the window.

"I'm glad we're finally getting to hang out, you know, not covered in meat," Andrew said with a teasing smile on his face.

"Oh, I'm still covered in meat. Washing my hands after work can only do so much."

"Well, it suits you then. I think you're cute, meat and all."

Annie blushed and took a sip of her coffee. So he was still interested. That made things more difficult. They talked about easy things – work, how another keeper almost let the chimps out of their enclosure, favorite foods – until Andrew asked when she was going home.

"Um, well, my job ends in two months so I'm only supposed to stay until the end of the summer."

Andrew swirled the dregs of his coffee around in his cup for a moment before responding.

"You should stay."

Annie felt more surprised by this than the kiss."

"Seriously. I could hire you fulltime. I like...working with you. You're a natural with the cats. Don't go back. Stay."

The sincerity in his eyes was overwhelming. It had only been a week but she had developed a strong connection with Andrew. They spent nearly every day together, just them and the cats. She knew she liked being around him, but she didn't realize how much until now. He reached out over the table and grabbed her rand, running his thumb softly over her palm. The electricity was back.

"You should stay."

She would stay. The decision she fretted over was made simple in that moment, even simpler than what she longed for back home. She'd stay in that coffee shop with him that evening – she didn't need to see Sean anymore – and she'd stay in the city with him chopping up bits of meat and tossing them to the big cats. She couldn't promise forever, it was too soon for that anyways, but she could promise now. Camilla might be the queen of the zoo, but Andrew made her feel like the queen of everything else.

BLISSFUL

ELOISE LEWIS

Annaleise rolled over in her cotton sheets and stared out the window at the sun beaming through the ragged curtains of her bedroom. The light from the morning lit up the interior of her modest room. The cock crowed as she stirred and stepped from the comfort of the warm bed. As her delicate toes touched the floor she winced at the feel of the cool floorboards beneath her feet. She mentally prepared herself for another typical day in the remote Amish community where she was raised. She sat on the edge of her bed and began braiding her long, golden locks. Her hair had never been cut. Once finished she tied a tiny, white bow at the end. Standing up, her hair extended all the way down to her upper thighs.

From the homely bedside table, she grabbed her prayer cap, the white cap made of organza and stiff with starch that she must wear in public. She slipped it over her long, golden braid and stood, making her way over to the wardrobe, barefoot. The floorboards creaked beneath her slender frame. The house in which she lived was in need of much repair, but it was home.

Her dress was bound by the Amish community to which she belonged. She pulled out the calf-length, gray dress, and her white apron to accompany it. She looked the outfit up and down, sighing at the restrictions she had to abide by. Just a little color or a little lace would make it so much more tolerable, but alas it was forbidden.

She slipped the dress over her head, atop the white, cotton undergarments she wore beneath. Her slender arms penetrated the long sleeves at the ends and her delicate fingers stretched out toward the floor. Her blue eyes reflected in the full-length mirror that stood opposite. They ran over her entire frame, assessing the modesty of her attire. Her smooth legs peeked out the bottom of the gown. Her hands just protruded from the sleeves. How she longed for something different. To have somewhat more choice when it came to the little things. But living here her options were overly restricted. With a sigh, she turned away from her dull reflection.

Her stomach growled lightly, alerting her that breakfast time was upon her. Before leaving, she quickly raced to the window and opened it wide, allowing the cool morning air to hit her face. It almost stung as the contrasting wind nipped at her warm skin. She turned on her heels and made her way to the exit of her humble sanctuary, ready to start the day ahead.

Before opening the door she took a deep breath, hearing the faint clip-clop of hooves outside. She felt a tear well up in the corner of her eye, but she willed it to stop. No matter how much she tried, Annaleise was overwhelmed with pain with any reminder of her parent's accident. No day since their passing had her parent's death become any easier for Annaleise. Each day she was reminded of the terrible accident they had undertaken. As soon as she set eyes on the cart outside, laying rusted and disheveled. Unused for a year. A constant visual scar, sitting in their front yard. Although she knew that her brother, Jacob, shared her pain she would not dare discuss with him.

He had been walking down the street when it occurred. On his way back from the cornfields down the road from their home. Their mother and father waved as they passed, smiling at him. The next thing Jacob knew, he was watching their cart overturn as the horses bucked and bolted, leaving the two bodies trapped beneath the wreckage. Around him, people screamed at the sight, but all he could do was rush over to find his parents laying lifeless in the middle of the dirt road.

Annaleise was distraught. She cried for weeks. She took to her room and moped. No one could comfort her. Since then the community had done their best to assist the two orphaned children. They stayed in the family home, but here they could barely make ends meet. Her job as a milkmaid at the dairy farm and his as an apprentice blacksmith left them living pay day to pay day. They relied on handouts from neighbors and friends to feed themselves. Still, Annaleise and Jacob vowed to take care of themselves, and that was just what they did. Regardless of if it was against the rules.

One evening, months after the accident, Jacob had an idea. He weighed it up in his mind over and over. He had promised Annaleise the day of their parents passing that he would always take care of her. That was just what he intended to do. But not if it meant risking her safety or standing within the community. Finally, he decided that there was no other option for them. The need for financial stability was too great.

"Come out with me tonight," he had asked, his voice trembling with what she felt to be nerves, excitement or worry, she could not distinguish.

"To where?" she had asked, but he would not answer. Annaleise was wary at first of her brother's sudden plan. Still, she trusted him and so she followed, through the woods and to the city on the other side.

"Where are we going, Jacob?" she asked on their journey. He turned and held out his hand, signaling her to stop in her tracks. He opened the knapsack he had been holding tightly to his chest since they had left the community. Inside was a range of colorful clothing, the likes of which Annaleise had never seen.

"I am taking you to the city," he explained, pulling out a pale pink fitted dress and white heels for his sister. She stared in awe at the strange fabric garments handed to her.

"You need to wear these, otherwise they will know we are not from there," he explained. Entering a modern city in their modest attire would surely give them away as patrons of the well-known Amish district just miles away. Jacob had experienced this prejudice first hand after all.

"I will stand over there. Let me know when you have changed. You can put your clothes in this bag," he gestured to the bag from which he had pulled the new outfit. Then he turned and walked out of sight, giving his sister the privacy to change.

She untied her apron and dropped her dress to the forest floor. She folded them and placed them in the knapsack Jacob had provided. She shivered in the cold night air. Picking up the new dress she pulled it gingerly over her head. It was so tight and firm around her body. She looked down at herself in the odd creation. Quickly she slipped the heels on her feet and called out,

"I think I am ready Jacob!" moments later he emerged from the shadows. He paused, taken aback by his sister's speedy transformation. He took her hand and kicked the knapsack into a large bush beside them.

"Time to go then," he whispered and they were off again through the trees.

When they came out on the other side of the vast wood, Annaleise stopped in awe. The lights glistened in the distance as they looked over the high-rise jungle. Jacob had been lucky enough to experience life on the other side. This is where he had been during Rumspringa, but his freedom was short-lived. He promptly returned to the community, overwhelmed by the progression he experienced.

Annaleise had not had that luxury. This was her first time in the city, even seeing it from a distance.

"Why are you bringing me here?" she mumbled. Jacob's expression became serious.

"We need money, Annaleise. I did not want to worry you with such matters but since our parents passing we have been struggling... more than you know." she had no idea what this had to do with going to the city.

"We can get jobs here. Second jobs, at night. It has been so hard for us Annaliese and I need your help. Please," he begged. But she would do anything for her brother. She took his hand once more and squeezed it kindly.

"Then let's go," she said, excitedly.

Months later and they had been working at the diner quite regularly, almost every night. Annaleise darted around in her short, yellow waitressing uniform, serving tables left and right. After her first day, she was amazed at how much money she had made, and just in tips. In the kitchen her brother worked hastily, cleaning dish after dish and piles of cutlery. But neither of them minded the hard work, especially Annaleise. She was happy to just be out in the real world.

"Order up!" the chef boomed from the service window. He rang the bell relentlessly to alert her of food being ready to pick up. She scooted over and took it to her waiting customers. Now she had everything down to a fine art.

The sneaking around was getting quite cumbersome, however. Her heart raced each night her and Jacob ventured out, against the communities wishes. That night when she got home she collapsed on the bed and stared up at the ceiling. Exhausted, she wished her life was more simple. Leading her dual existence was taking its toll on her. She was plagued with a lack of sleep and a crippling anxiety. Tossing and turning during her few hours sleep each night. Alas, she had no other choice, for now anyway. She felt a huge debt weighing on her, for her brother. He had taken care of Annaleise since their parent's sudden demise. No matter how much she wished she could leave, it was not an option.

One morning as she was walking down the street, Annaleise was greeted by an unexpected face.

"Annaleise!" a man's voice boomed from behind her. She turned quickly on her heel to see an old friend, one whom she thought had left for good years earlier.

"Jebidiah?" she said, stunned. Her grocery basket fell to the ground with a thud as she ran toward him and wrapped her arms around his broad shoulders. He picked her up around the waist and they held their embrace for several seconds. Even though it had been so long since their last encounter, neither failed to recognize the other.

He dropped her back to the ground and she stepped back slightly to take in the sight of her long lost friend. His hair was styled just as it always had been. His dark brown locks were cut short, a few inches from his scalp. It hung in waves around his face. His skin was tanned and contrasted perfectly with his strong, masculine jawline and muscular figure. His chin was littered with stubble, giving his face a slight shadowing.

Their last meeting had not been so joyous. Jebidiah had been leaving for Rumspringa with her brother Jacob. The three children had grown up as close as they could be, spending endless hours together playing in the cornfields and chasing each other through the streets. Since the age of five, Annaleise and Jebidiah had known each other. She saw him as one of her closest friends. Or at least she had before he disappeared.

It had been a cold night, pelting down with rain. They stood there, facing each other. Annaleise had been fifteen, Jebidiah sixteen. Not a word was spoken for several minutes between them. Too young to realize the deep feelings that connected them, Jebidiah left with Jacob, to experience the modern world with the rest of the community boys coming of age that year. Annaleise had waited for him. She waited up at night and watched for him during the day. But he did not return.

Jacob came back weeks later with a few of the neighborhood boys, but Jebidiah was not among them.

Her brother had rested his hand on her shoulder as tears rolled down her face, tears for the loss of her best friend.

"He said to tell you he will see you again. He promised." at the time Annaleise had not believed him. She had thought her brother was trying desperately to bring her out of her deepening hole of overwhelming sadness. But with Jebidiah standing before her, Jacob's words echoed in the midst of her thoughts.

'He promised.'

She had given up hope of seeing him again, yet here he stood, in the flesh.

Jebidiah was speechless. He had returned to the community after years. It seemed that no matter how much the modern world drew him, his love for Annaleise was stronger. From the day he had left, he did not stop thinking about her, not for a moment. It had been fun and he savored the new experiences put forth by his peers in the city, but no one could replace her. That was what influenced him to return. There was nothing more he could gain from the city, he was looking to start a family. Jebidiah could not consider anyone else he would rather make a life with than her.

"I hope Jacob gave you my message all those years ago," he said, smiling down at her from above.

"He did," she replied, mirroring the beam that had taken over Jebidiah's face. Any onlooker could tell that these two were much more than just friends, even if they had not yet admitted it to themselves. They still grasped the hands of each other as they chatted for a few minutes about shared memories from the past.

Jebidiah bent down and picked up the discarded basket of groceries Annaleise had dropped in her shock at his appearance.

"Let's go for a walk, I need to catch up with you. So much has happened in the last few years I am sure," he laughed. As they strolled along they spoke at length about their experiences. Everything Jebidiah said about his time away absolutely intrigued her. She desperately wished that she could share in this modern world, if only for a day. Working was all she had ever had the chance to do when her and Jacob managed to escape for their night shifts.

"So, what about your life, Annaleise?" he questioned. After a moment of thought, he saw her face drop. The only significant thing she could think of to tell him was of her parent's sudden demise the previous fall. She took a deep breath and prepared herself for the retelling of the most painful memory she possessed.

"Actually, there was an accident last year," she began. Jebidiah's permanent grin faded almost immediately.

"My parents cart overturned. It was terrifying but the worst was that they did not make it." Jebidiah could not find the words to express his condolences. After a few moments to comprehend the brief and saddening story he mustered,

"I am so sorry, Annaleise."

As always, her first thought was to change the subject, and so she did. Long ago she had decided that her parents would not have wanted her to mourn, but cherish the life that she had. That was exactly what she intended to do. The sadness they had been wallowing in for that brief moment evaporated quickly as they moved on to more trivial and light-hearted news from their vast time apart.

Jebidiah walked her all the way back to her door. He handed back the basket as she stepped through the threshold of the dark, polished doorway.

"Well, I am sure we will see each other again soon," he said as he turned to leave.

"You will," she smiled and with that the door clicked shut behind her.

As the following months flew by, Annaleise found herself spending more and more of her limited free time with her long lost friend. Jebidiah found comfort in their closeness. Since moving back, he had faced endless scrutiny from the older members of the place he called home. They frowned upon him for his rash decision to leave, now that he had returned. He had known upon his abrupt return to his family that not everyone would be so welcoming. But no one else mattered as long as Annaleise was by his side.

She found comfort in his company too. She was intrigued by his endless stories of the new technologies and strange architecture he had encountered in his years away. Unlike her peers, Annaleise held nothing against him for leaving, if anything she wished that she could do the same.

The two companions spent their time just as they did, years earlier. Exploring the now familiar woods. Chasing each other through the cornfields. Collapsing with laughter on the dirt floor of the outdoors.

They savored each moment they spent in each others company. To Annaleise, no one could compare to Jebidiah.

One sunny afternoon, they fell into each other's arms in the dewy grass of the outskirts of the boundary. Their laughter subsided and Annaleise looked up at Jebidiah, beaming down at her. She knew that there was something deeper. This was not just another friendship, he meant so much more. Every second without him left her feeling cold and empty. Every second without her made him feel as if he was completely alone.

"Do you think you will stay here this time?" Annaleise asked. She hoped that his answer reflected the way that she felt. But alas, he uttered the answer she did not want to hear.

"No. I think that now I have experienced what is out there, lived my life outside the confines of the community, I don't want to leave again." her heart dropped. There was nothing in the world she wished for more than to go, but a life without Jebidiah seemed just as empty.

It was his strength that encouraged her to plan her escape, to a new life in the modern world. Deep in her heart she knew that it was unlikely Jebidiah would come with her. After all, he had returned not weeks ago, but she had to follow her dreams. She had but one life, and she intended to live it. As much as she wanted to share with him her wishes, she knew this was one secret she must keep to herself.

Jebidiah walked her home again that day, as he often did of late. The sun was setting over the sovereign hills as they strolled past people and places on the way home. She took in the sights, for in a few weeks they would be gone forever. There was no doubt she would miss this place, but most of all she would miss him. She cherished the time they had together, though short lived.

They arrived at her home. Before she opened the door, Jebidiah grasped her wrist tightly. Her skin broke out in goosebumps all over in response to his flesh against hers. Her heart raced within her chest cavity. Cheeks began to glow red as the blood from her pounding heart rushed to her face. She hoped that Jebidiah did not see the intense reaction she gave from his touch.

"Do you have plans for tomorrow?" he questioned. His expression was serious all of a sudden.

"No," Annaleise responded. Where was he going with this?

"I see, well goodnight then," he said with a grin. How strange. With that Jebidiah let go of her arm and placed his hands into his pockets.

"Goodbye," she called to him as he strolled slowly away, toward his family home at the end of the road.

As she closed the door behind her Annaleise leaned her back against the rough wood and closed her eyes. The overwhelming sensation of lust she felt for Jebidiah was quickly blooming into a raging passion. Love. Little did she know that he felt it too. From the top of her head to the far tips of her toes her entire being was filled with admiration and desire for him. How would she tell him that she was going to leave the town? Start a new life in the place that he had run from.

She already had a plan in place. Two weeks from now she would be living amongst the modern world. Jacob had not been pleased, but he knew that he could not stop his sister from following her dreams. He had the opportunity, so there was no way that he could deny her that right, regardless of the community law.

"Are you sure you will be OK on your own?" Jacob could not hide the worried tone of his voice. Not even he could brave the new world, how could his little sister live there alone?

"I will, please do not worry about me, Jacob," then she explained her plan.

In the dead of night, while the town slept, she would sneak silently through the streets. Toward the wood. The path that they had traveled hundreds of times before would lead her to her new existence. She could not leave during the day, for fear of what scrutiny she may face from the others in the town. Women rarely left and were never welcomed home. It was best for her to just disappear.

"But you have never been that way alone." he said, his voice still trembling with fear for Annaleise.

"I have mapped out our way. The last few weeks I have made a note of each landmark along the path. Each time I feel as if my feet lead me more and more. I step without hesitation." slowly she had memorized the way. Every rock and tree, branch and shrub. The dirt clearings and the overgrown mangling of tangled weeds, she was confident in her navigational ability. Even if Jacob was not so.

"Where will you stay?" his questions kept coming. But Annaleise was not one to take her decisions lightly. To his every question, she had the perfect answer. During their time at the diner, they had made a few friends, both co-workers, and customers. Annaleise had organized a room in a modest apartment with Katie, a fellow waitress at a neighboring restaurant. For only a small portion of her minimum wage, she had a place to her her own.

Several hours later, Annaleise had assured her brother that she could fend for herself. If she ever needed him, he would be there for her too.

Jacob took her hand and looked at her, eyes full of sadness.

"I will always be here for you, sister," a single tear rolled down his cheek, winding its way through the stubble on his strong chin. Annaleise was taken aback, she had not seen her brother so emotional since their parents passing. She whispered the only words that came to mind in response to his heartfelt confession.

"I know," tears now flowed freely down their faces. They sat in silence as Jacob took in the news she had revealed to him. The plan she had derived. How much he would miss her.

The hardest part was over. Annaleise had dreaded telling her brother about her escape. Now she felt free, with his blessing she could leave without hesitation. She slept that night, soundly for the first time in many moons. Dreaming of the future adventures she would have in the big city.

The next morning Jebidiah was at her door before either of the siblings had risen. She heard the light tapping from her bedroom and quickly dressed to see who was so desperate to see them this day. She raced down the creaking steps and to the front door. Opening it widely she was ecstatic to see Jebidiah standing there with a bouquet of red roses. Their scent was swept immediately into her nostrils and she closed her eyes as the aroma intoxicated her.

"Good morning, Annaleise," Jebidiah greeted her, placing the stunning bunch into her hands.

"Hello," she replied, staring at the gift he had brought for her. Something was different about him this morning. She could not pick it but his smile was strange somehow, brighter than she had seen before. His eyes sparkled in the morning light. Her heart skipped a beat as they paused for a moment, looking deeply into each other's eyes.

"I have a day planned for us," he said excitedly. Before she had time to properly lace up her boots, Jebidiah took her hand and whisked her away from her home. They walked together toward the vast cornfields at the end of the street. Waving at their fellow community members as they passed, Jebidiah led Annaleise through the tall corn stalks.

She had no idea what he had in store. They rushed forward in silence. Annaleise found her mind wandering as she took in the rays of sunlight winding through the stalks and leaves surrounding them. Her dress occasionally caught on rouge sticks and branches strewn throughout the fields. She stumbled a few times, but Jebidiah was there to catch her and help her find her feet once more.

Minutes passed and they finally arrived at the small clearing in the far end of the fields. Jebidiah let her hand drop and pulled a blanket from the backpack he had been lugging with them on the short journey. He laid it delicately out on the ground, straightening the edges and patting it down flat.

"Come, sit," he gestured to a soft spot on the blanket and she slowly approached, sitting down carefully, holding her dress flat against her thighs as she lowered her body to the ground. She watched on as Jebidiah began unpacking a picnic that he had prepared. She was stunned at the romantic setting that he had created for just the two of them, out of nowhere.

"I hope you're hungry," he laughed. Her eyes drifted from plate to plate, each piled high with sandwiches and cakes, fruit and salads. She could not believe what she saw before her. This was the kind of thing she had always dreamed of but had never eventuated into a reality. The sun beamed down on them as they began their conversations.

"Please," Jebidiah picked up a plate of her favorite sandwiches, fresh strawberry jam. She picked up one and took a bite. The sweetness of the jam found every corner of her tongue, leaving a lasting sensation in her mouth as she swallowed. He watched her intently, looking as if something was weighing heavily on his mind. Annaleise looked into his deep, brown eyes. She felt herself smile as she took in his handsome features, just inches from her. His short, dark hair flowed subtly in the mild breeze. Her gaze followed his masculine jawline and rugged chin, covered in light stubble.

It was at that moment Jebidiah uttered the words she had been longing for him to say for so long,

"I love you, Annaleise, I always have." she was taken aback. Of course, her heart reciprocated his feelings, but she could not bring herself to say the words back. In the back of her mind, she knew that if she revealed her love for him she must also let him in on the fact she was planning to leave. Leave him and everything else behind. Moments later she found her voice once more,

"I love you too."

They spoke for hours after Jebidiah's unexpected, but heartfelt, confession. Of life and the paths they wanted to take in the future. That was when troubles arose.

"I just want to settle down, and have a family. I love it so much here. It feels so right to be back." Jebidiah said in between bites of his rosy red apple. Annaleise froze. This was exactly the life she was running from. It was the first time that she realized that their journeys may lead them in different directions. She sat silent for a moment as he waited patiently for her to say something, anything. She took a deep breath and proceeded to reveal her underlying plan to Jebidiah. Her plan to leave and start a new life in the city he had fled from.

"I had no idea," Jebidiah gasped, in response to her and Jacob's secret second existence outside of the community. His heart dropped as she continued to explain her plans to escape and live amongst the modern world. Never had he thought coming into the fields with her that morning that she would drop this bombshell upon him. All hopes of his quiet life back at home with his childhood sweetheart were slowly evaporating before his eyes.

"When do you plan to leave?" he questioned, his heartbeat pounding in his chest. He prayed that it was not soon. That he would have time to change her mind.

"Two weeks from today," she admitted. His smile had faded, and hers with it. She had thought that the hardest conversation before her departure was over, but she had not counted on Jebidiah's romantic notions. His proposal of a simple, family life in the mundane town she had always lived. She loved him deeply, but her want for adventure was overwhelming.

With the sun beginning to lower over the tips of the corn, they decided that it was time to return. She folded the blanket as Jebidiah picked up the empty plates that surrounded them in the clearing. He took her hand and led the way back through the towering stalks. They moved at a much slower pace upon their return. Annaleise could not be sure, maybe it was due to the dimming light, but she felt as if their lagging pace was a bi-product of the conversations they had just had. Of her leaving him and the rest of her life behind.

Eventually, they reached her front door once more. She stepped up the front stair and peered down at him.

"Thank you for today, Jebidiah. I had an amazing time. I really appreciate all that you have done for me," Annaleise checked quickly for onlookers and before a word could escape his lips she kissed him tenderly on the cheek. By the time Jebidiah realized what had happened she had already stepped back inside.

He began his journey home, filled with mixed emotions from the day just passed. He desperately wanted Annaleise to stay, but he understood her position was difficult. With constant reminders daily of her parent's death, he could only imagine the heartache she must feel living here.

Two weeks later, the grandfather clock below the stairs began chiming midnight. Annaleise knew this was her chance to make her escape quietly, without fear of waking her sleeping neighborhood. She tiptoed down the stairs, their echoing creaks masked by the gongs of the great timekeeper. Her blonde locks fell over her face as she looked down toward the door, her destination on this dark winter night. She brushed them aside and kept moving. Grabbing the already assembled knapsack from its hiding spot, she slipped her pale pink coat over her slender shoulders and on the final stroke of midnight the door clicked shut behind her.

The cool wind bit at her exposed flesh as she crept through the dead of night. She knew that by leaving she was breaking her oath to the Church, but the call of the outside world was just too great. Not even her one true love could keep her from following her dreams. A single tear rolled slowly down her pale cheek as she looked back, back at the friends and family she would no longer see. Back at Jebidiah.

Tearing her gaze away she strove forward. Her hair was now wet with sweat, despite the cold air that stung her face and pierced her lungs. She ran, as fast as she could. Each snapping twig made her heart jump. Every sound around her made her pause for a moment. A moment was all she could spare. Slowly she kept moving, through the woods, following the hidden road to freedom. As she made her way Annaleise found her mind wandering back to all of her most cherished memories with the community and everything she was giving up. The celebrations and family dinners. Just as she lost herself completely in her thoughts a sharp noise snapped her back to reality.

She looked around desperately for somewhere to hide. She could distinguish faint footsteps coming her way. Who could be out here this late, in the cold? Annaleise was convinced that she was caught. Someone had overheard her speaking of her plan to Jebidiah, or worse he had outed her himself. She threw her knapsack into a large bush to her left and jumped behind. As she crouched on the ground crazy accusations filled her head, but she kept her blue eyes focused on the clearing before her. Was it Jebidiah who let slip her secret plan, or did someone else overhear? When a shadowy figure finally caught her eye in the woods, she waited with baited breath to identify her stalker.

Branches crunched beneath his feet as the man emerged into the grassy clearing, uncloaked by the light of the moon. Annaleise's jaw dropped and her heart raced at what felt like a thousand beats a second. She no longer needed to hide, she no longer had any fear or doubt about the path that she had chosen.

"Jebidiah!" she exclaimed, sprinting as fast as her legs could carry her toward him. A smile exploded across his face as she jumped carelessly into his outstretched arms. Jebidiah wrapped his muscular arms around her. He grasped her as tight as he could, never wanting to part again. She let her body melt into his. There they stood, nestled in each other's arms for several moments before severing their sensual embrace.

"I could not let you go, Annaleise. I love you." Jebidiah confessed. She stared into his beaming blue eyes, looking down upon her. There was only one thing that she could respond.

"I love you too," she answered. Her eyes welled up with blissful tears that soon began running, one by one, down her soft cheeks. Jebidiah reached forward and wiped them away with his calloused hands. One of her arms drew back, reaching up to run her fingers through his mess of tangled hair, damp with sweat. Still stunned by his sudden appearance, she was nothing but ecstatic to see him.

At that moment, Jebidiah leaned down and kissed her soft, cherry lips for the first time, basking in the cool blanket of moonlight penetrating the canopy. Annaleise could not believe her luck as she stood in the middle of the trees, in the arms of her love. She had been sure, not hours ago, that she had lost the love of her life forever. Now, she was on her way to making a new life for herself, in a new world, with the man of her dreams.

She leaned in closer to his warm silhouette, grasping at the fabric of his coat. She savored his touch, something she thought she had lost forever in the sands of time. His hand brushed her now flushing cheeks. He traced down her neck and over her petite shoulder. Her hand found its place against his pounding chest. And hers against his.

Jebidiah brushed a lock of hair from Annaleise's ear.

"We must go now," he whispered softly to her. Stepping back from him, she nodded in agreement. She would no longer need to start her new life alone, they were together at last. He picked up her knapsack and hauled it onto his back.

"Come," he ushered Annaleise back onto her path. Toward the city for the last time. As they neared the bustling hub, she witnessed the blanket of light illuminating the town. Never had she seen something so beautiful. Never had she felt so free.

www.ingramcontent.com/pod-product-compliance
Lightning Source LLC
Chambersburg PA
CBHW030334160726
47987CB00021B/498